COOL MATH

Math Tricks,
Amazing Math Activities,
Cool Calculations,
Awesome Math Factoids,
and More

Written by Christy Maganzini
Illustrated by Ruta Daugavietis

PRICE STERN SLOAN

For the Maganzini boys: Erminio, Andy, George, and Aldo
—C.M.

Acknowledgements
Special thanks to Ronn Yablun, winner of the LACTMA Outstanding Math Teacher Award, for his review on the project. He is the author of *Mathamazement* and *How to Develop Your Child's Gifts and Talents in Math*. Thanks also goes to "Dr. Zee" Zondra Knapp for her very helpful suggestions. Zondra has been a California Mentor Teacher and has worked as a curriculum consultant for the California Department of Education.

Edited by Lisa Rojany, Catherine Stringer,
Melinda Thompson, Daniel Weizmann, and Windy Just
Copyright © 1997 RGA Publishing Group, Inc.
Published by Price Stern Sloan, Inc.
A member of The Putnam & Grosset Group, New York, New York.

ISBN: 0-8431-7857-4
First Edition
1 3 5 7 9 10 8 6 4 2

Library of Congress Cataloging-in-Publication Data

Maganzini, Christy.
    Cool math / by Christy Maganzini ;
illustrated by Ruta Daugavietis. -- 1st ed.
        p. cm.
    Includes index.
    Summary: Describes mathematics from zero to infinity with stops along the way for ancient puzzles, awesome math tricks, tantalizing math trivia, incredible shortcuts, and mysterious number magic.
    ISBN 0-8431-7857-4
    1. Mathematics--Juvenile literature. [1. Mathematics.]
I. Daugavietis, Ruta. II. Title.
QA40.5.M34 1997
510--dc21

                                                              96-40484
                                                                  CIP
                                                                   AC

CONTENTS

Contents

WHAT'S SO COOL ABOUT MATH?

There isn't a kid on the planet who hasn't felt his or her brain go numb while practicing multiplication tables. You've all stared at colorful pictures of a sliced-up pizza to learn about **fractions**, which are numbers that show a part's relationship to the whole. This type of math, whether it's about fractions or not, we'll call "pizza math."

The sad truth about pizza math is this: A lot of kids become bored with it. They decide that if math is just about doing problem after problem after problem . . . well, forget it. They'll do the worksheets, but there is no way that math is going to be their favorite subject—ever. This is too bad, because once you get past the "pizza" phase of it, math can seriously boggle your brain.

For instance, think about some cool inventions that we can use every day, such as pocket-sized pagers, virtual reality games, and the Internet. Did you know that these inventions required people to use imagination, creativity, daring, and . . . numbers?

Up until now, everyone figured kids just couldn't handle certain mathematical ideas because, well, they were kids and they were better off doing lots and lots of pizza math to keep their "little minds" busy. But the imagination of even the most average kid is a very powerful thing.

When you explore the world of mathematics, a good imagination will take you very far—maybe even to the edge of the universe. How? Look at it this way: How could you even begin to think about something like infinity if you didn't have an imagination? How could you possibly contemplate the value of *pi* if you couldn't use your imagination? Keep in mind that you can't physically touch numbers, nor can you smell, hear, or taste them! But numbers serve a very important purpose—to symbolize and represent important ideas from the **B.C.E.** (that's Before Common Era) generation up through today, and they have done so for thousands of years.

We are going to take you from **zero** to *infinity* with stops along the way for ancient puzzles, awesome math tricks, tantalizing math trivia, incredible shortcuts, and mysterious number magic. And we even make it easier for you by *bolding* new terms that you can look up in the glossary at the back of the book or by defining them right there in the text. So get ready to see math as you've never seen it before! Get ready for *Cool Math!*

Please Take a Number: From Zero to Googolplex

As I was going to St. Ives,
I met a man with seven wives,
Every wife had seven sacks,
Every sack had seven cats,
Every cat had seven kits,
Kits, cats, sacks, and wives,
How many were going to St. Ives?

—18th century nursery rhyme

The brainteaser above just happens to be the oldest number puzzle in the world. An almost identical version appears on an ancient Egyptian scroll containing several arithmetic problems and number tables. Historians discovered that the scroll was written in 1650 B.C.E.! (Do you think you know the answer to the brainteaser? Turn to page 94 to see if you're right!)

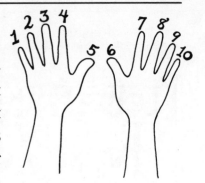

That ancient riddle helps to make a point: Before there was mathematics, there was counting. Archaeologists have found evidence that prehistoric peoples from 30,000 years ago cut notches in bones to keep track of things. Perhaps those things were animals they had captured for food. Way back then, when there weren't even *names* for numbers, people understood that one notch stood for one animal, two notches for two, and so on. When you think of your own experience with numbers, it probably also started with counting—fingers, toes, scabs, whatever.

After you learned to count, you discovered numerals and **place value**, which is the amount a digit is worth based on its placement in a number. Our number system is based on the number 10 and is called a **base 10 number system**. This means that all our place values are powers of 10. (See these "powers" at work on pages 14 and 15.) We have a place value for ones (1), a place value for tens (10 x 1), a place value for hundreds (10 x 10), a place value for thousands (10 x 10 x 10), a place value for ten thousands (10 x 10 x 10 x 10), and so on.

The ancient peoples spent over 27,000 years developing their number system. By 1795 B.C.E. the Babylonians (a very old civilization that existed in the country that is now called Iraq) had developed a number system and even created a type of counting board, called an **abacus**. When shopkeepers tallied a bill, they placed these counting boards on a table called a "counter." The picture at the left shows what an abacus looks like.

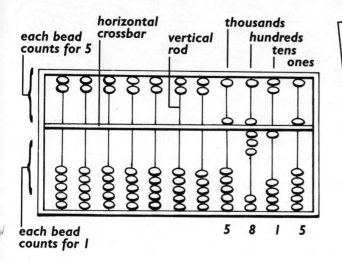

each bead counts for 5 | horizontal crossbar | vertical rod | thousands | hundreds | tens | ones

each bead counts for 1

5 8 1 5

MATH MILESTONES: ALL ABOUT ABACI

Ancient peoples all around the globe were found to have used abacuses, or *abaci* (AB-uh-seye)—Chinese, Egyptians, and the Mayan Indians in Central and South America. Abaci are still used in many parts of Asia. Some people are so fast with an abacus they can beat a pocket calculator in reaching an answer!

Here are the basics on how to use an abacus:

Each vertical rod represents a place value. Starting from the right, the first rod represents the "ones" place, the second rod stands for the "tens" place, the third rod shows the "hundreds" place, and so on. The beads beneath the horizontal crossbar count for one each. The beads above the horizontal crossbar count for five each. To calculate on an abacus, first clear it so that no beads touch the crossbar. Then feed in the first number simply by sliding the corresponding bead or beads to the center bar. The abacus above shows the number 5,815.

What came after counting, numerals, and number systems is what this book is all about: mathematics, the science of numbers. Mathematics is not about adding, subtracting, multiplying, or dividing. It's about studying numbers as if they were some kind of crazy science project. It's about solving problems. And if you can't imagine numbers getting absolutely, totally wild, hang on to your high-tops: It's time to meet the Greeks. When it came to mathematics, they *rocked*. The ancient Greeks in 500 B.C.E. were fascinated by numbers. To some of them, mathematics was practically a religion. In fact, one Greek philosopher and mathematician, **Pythagorus** (puh-THA-guh-ruhs), *did* make it something of a religion.

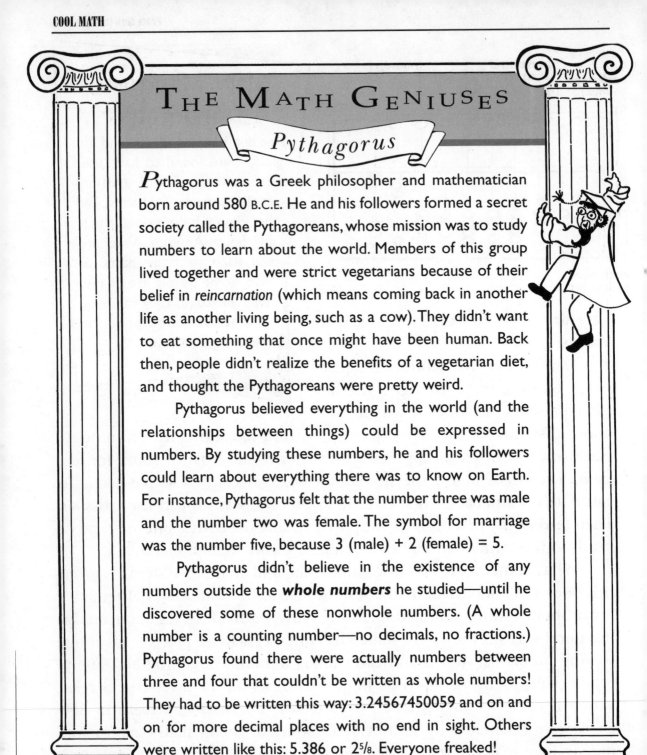

THE MATH GENIUSES
Pythagorus

*P*ythagorus was a Greek philosopher and mathematician born around 580 B.C.E. He and his followers formed a secret society called the Pythagoreans, whose mission was to study numbers to learn about the world. Members of this group lived together and were strict vegetarians because of their belief in *reincarnation* (which means coming back in another life as another living being, such as a cow). They didn't want to eat something that once might have been human. Back then, people didn't realize the benefits of a vegetarian diet, and thought the Pythagoreans were pretty weird.

Pythagorus believed everything in the world (and the relationships between things) could be expressed in numbers. By studying these numbers, he and his followers could learn about everything there was to know on Earth. For instance, Pythagorus felt that the number three was male and the number two was female. The symbol for marriage was the number five, because 3 (male) + 2 (female) = 5.

Pythagorus didn't believe in the existence of any numbers outside the **whole numbers** he studied—until he discovered some of these nonwhole numbers. (A whole number is a counting number—no decimals, no fractions.) Pythagorus found there were actually numbers between three and four that couldn't be written as whole numbers! They had to be written this way: 3.24567450059 and on and on for more decimal places with no end in sight. Others were written like this: 5.386 or 2⅝. Everyone freaked!

The discovery of "nonwhole" numbers caused a big ruckus because it challenged the earlier teachings of Pythagorus. Was it possible the math master had made a boo-boo? The Pythagoreans swore each other to secrecy, under penalty of death. Unfortunately, word got out. One member of the group was found dead a short time later. He had apparently drowned. Was it accidental? Or had he blabbed the BIG SECRET?

Lucky for us, math isn't quite so risky nowadays. Although the Pythagoreans were disbanded in a political uprising, the study of numbers begun by the Babylonians and ancient Greeks was the starting point for mathematics as we know it today.

Since the science of mathematics began with numbers, that's where we'll start. Let's take a look at a number that was named over 200 years after the others. The name of this Johnny-come-lately is zero.

What if there was no zero?

Look! A Quadrilateral!

Before the invention of the number zero (about 1,500 years ago), how did people write numbers like **200** or **202**? People showed a missing place value by leaving the space empty. Using this method, the number **202** might have looked like this: **2 2**. What if the number were **2,002**? It looked like this: **2   2**. It's easy to see that with this type of system, one number could easily be mistaken for another. What if we didn't have the number zero today? Can you think of some ways to write the number **200** without using zero?

You could write the words: **two hundred**.

You could use *Roman numerals:* **CC**.

You could write a math sentence like this: **2 x 5 x 2 x 5 x 2**

or like this: **199 + 1**

or like this: **299 − 99**.

Or if you had a lot of time on your hands, you could write out a lot of chicken scratches:

. . . but it sure wastes a lot more space, not to mention pencil lead. See how useful a zero can be?

The Number Zero: A Short Story About Nothing

It was a long, hot car ride across the desert and my mind ached from boredom. "Lunch time!" Dad announced as he slowed the family roast-mobile into the dusty parking lot of a roadside burger joint.

A faded sign boasted *"Over 2,000,000,000,000 served!"* Each zero had been stuck on the sign with a small nail. Was that 2 million, 20 million, or 2 billion? My brother insisted it was 2 jillion. I counted 12 zeros and immediately recognized the number as 2 trillion. I watched as one of the zeros blew off in the dry desert wind. Now the burger sign read "2,000,000,000,00." After mentally rearranging a few commas, I read the numbers as a mere 200 billion. How many burger sales did that one missing zero take with it? The figure was awesome—1 trillion, 800 billion burgers gone! A difference of over hundreds of billions of burgers with the loss of one zero. Yikes! Maybe that wasn't the first zero to blow away. Had there been more? The larger the original number, the greater the loss. *Zero* was definitely not *nothing*. It was *something*—something big. The number had taken hold of my brain.

Very Large Numbers: Wrestling with Giants

Enormous numbers can seem a little scary. No, we're not talking about big numbers like this:

2

We're talking about really *long* numbers like this:

2,667,000,442

Maybe it's all those zeros or commas that make these numeric behemoths so intimidating. It doesn't help that these heavyweights have a reputation for being difficult to work with, especially if you have a short attention span. People tend to stay far away from long numbers if they can. One look at all those digits, and most people shake their heads and say, "Hmmmm. Well, that's a pretty big number. You want me to do *what* with it?" There's usually a long, quiet pause. Then they remember they have some really important chores to do.

Sure, big numbers can be monsters, but they don't *mean* to be scary. They can't help being large, any more than you can help being irresistibly good-looking, charming, and intelligent. In time, you'll find that you actually need these giants. Why? Because if you want your world to be bigger, if you want to expand your horizons and reach for the quasars, you've got to know how to hang with the very big guys. We're talking **googols** and **googolplexes** here. Read on to learn what these weird-sounding numbers are.

Exponents Make Things Easier

One of the reasons people are so afraid of big numbers is because they're not sure of the difference between a million and a billion, a trillion, or a quintillion. It's true that after a while, all those zeros tend to blur together. There *is* a solution. You know how to write "USA" for the United States of America, and "RSVP" for *"Répondez s'il vous plaît"* (which really means "Let us know if you're coming to the party so we'll have enough pizza"). Surprise! Numbers can be abbreviated, too. The secret word is **exponent**. An exponent is a smaller-sized number written just above and to the right of a **base** number.

$$10^9 \quad \leftarrow \text{exponent}$$
$$\leftarrow \text{base}$$

An exponent tells how many base numbers to multiply. The example above can be read as "Ten to the 9th power," which is the same as multiplying 10 nine times, like this:

10 x 10 x 10 x 10 x 10 x 10 x 10 x 10 x 10 = 1,000,000,000 (1 billion)

$2 \times 2 \times 2 + 6 = \mathbf{14}$

Notice that when working with powers of 10, the exponent tells you how many zeros to write. There are 9 zeros in 1 billion; 9 was also shown as the exponent. (This nifty trick only works with the base number 10.)

Speaking of billions, do you know what to call the number that comes after 1 billion? This table shows you the names of numbers from 1 billion to 1 vigintillion. If you want to see what each number looks like without using an exponent, just take out a pencil and paper. Write a "1" and then add the number of zeros shown in the exponent on the table.

Number name	Written with an exponent	
Billion	10^9	
Trillion	10^{12}	(or 1 thousand billion)
Quadrillion	10^{15}	(or 1 million billion)
Quintillion	10^{18}	(or 1 billion billion)
Sextillion	10^{21}	(or 1 thousand billion billion)
Septillion	10^{24}	(or 1 million billion billion)
Octillion	10^{27}	(or 1 billion billion billion)
Nonillion	10^{30}	(or 1 thousand billion billion billion)
Decillion	10^{33}	(or 1 million billion billion billion)
Undecillion	10^{36}	(or 1 billion billion billion billion)
Duodecillion	10^{39}	(or 1 thousand billion billion billion billion)
Tredecillion	10^{42}	(or 1 million billion billion billion billion)
Quattuordecillion	10^{45}	(or 1 billion billion billion billion billion)
Quindecillion	10^{48}	(or 1 thousand billion billion billion billion billion)
Sexdecillion	10^{51}	(or 1 million billion billion billion billion billion)
Septendecillion	10^{54}	(or 1 billion billion billion billion billion billion)
Octodecillion	10^{57}	(or 1 thousand billion billion billion billion billion billion)
Novemdecillion	10^{60}	(or 1 million billion billion billion billion billion billion)
Vigintillion	10^{63}	(or 1 billion billion billion billion billion billion billion)

10^{66} GLIGILLION ???
10^{69} WILLIAMILLION ???
10^{72} UMBUSILLION ???
10^{75} NOILLILLION ???...

Are You Ready for the Googol?

Take this quiz and pick the letter that best fits.

A googol is: (pick one)

      a. something you dress up as for Halloween.

      b. a new kind of candy with gooey stuff in the center.

      c. the number 10^{100}.

If you answered "c," you're right! The googol, named in 1938 by nine-year-old Milton Sirotta (whose Uncle Edward happened to be a mathematician), is the number one with a hundred zeros written after it. A googol looks like this:

10,000,000,000,000,000,000,000,000,000, 000,000,000,000,000,000,000,000,000,000, 000,000,000,000,000,000,000,000,000,000, 000,000,000,000

Go ahead and count them. There really *are* 100 zeros there!

And, as if the googol weren't mind-boggling enough, Milton went on to name an even larger number—the spectacular, the unimaginable, the gargantuan—the googolplex. A googolplex is a one with a googol of zeros after it. You could also say it's a 10 to the googoleth power. To write it in exponential form:

$$\text{Googolplex} = 10^{googol} \text{ or } 10^{10^{100}}$$

Now you can see how using exponents saves you from a bad case of writer's cramp. But would you ever need to write such large numbers? Is there a googolplex of anything in the whole universe? Possibly. You never know when a googolplex of *something* might show up, and it's best to be prepared. By the way, the numbers between vigintillion and googol are still unnamed. What would you call them?

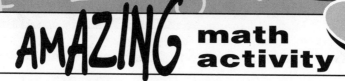

Playing with Palindromes

Read these words forward, then backward.

NOON   LEVEL   MOM   DAD

Now try reading the following sentences forward, then backward.

MADAM IM ADAM

A MAN A PLAN A CANAL PANAMA

Sentences, words, or numbers that read the same way forward and backward are called *palindromes*. It's a lot of fun making up palindromes, and the wackier the better! One of the longest and wildest palindromes (complete with punctuation) was created by a man named Jon Agee. It reads:

GO HANG A SALAMI! IM A LASAGNA HOG

You can have number palindromes, too. For example:

101   1221   438,834   123,456,654,321

Here's a really cool fact about number palindromes: You always get a palindrome when you add any number to its reverse twin (though it may take a few steps). Try it!

1. Pick your favorite three-digit number. How about your telephone area code? Let's say you live in Hollywood, California, where the area code is 213. ➡️

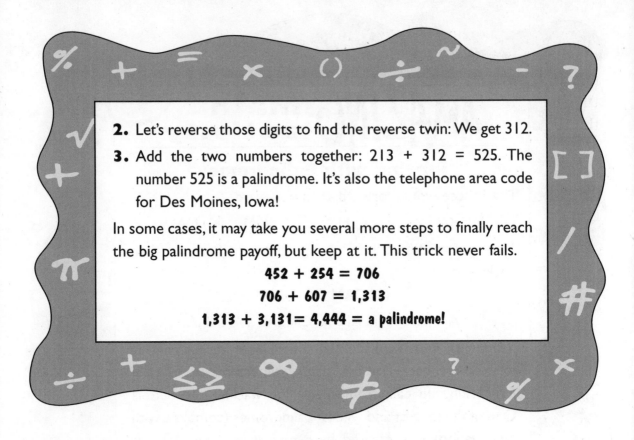

2. Let's reverse those digits to find the reverse twin: We get 312.

3. Add the two numbers together: 213 + 312 = 525. The number 525 is a palindrome. It's also the telephone area code for Des Moines, Iowa!

In some cases, it may take you several more steps to finally reach the big palindrome payoff, but keep at it. This trick never fails.

$$452 + 254 = 706$$
$$706 + 607 = 1,313$$
$$1,313 + 3,131 = 4,444 = \text{a palindrome!}$$

Less than Zero:
The Wacky World of Negative Numbers

Poor, misunderstood negative numbers have a reputation for being crabby, but they're not! Even though the word *negative* can describe a cranky person, when it is used to describe a number, it has a totally different meaning. A  **negative number** is simply a number that has a value less than zero, and has a minus sign written before it to show that it's negative. That's it!

If you've ever loaned a friend some coins to play a video game, you know how useful negative numbers can be. For example, a friend who owes you $5 has −$5 or "negative five" dollars. Negative numbers give us a way to write quantities less than zero. This is the same way banks keep track of their accounts. When we say someone's account is "in the red," it means he or she has a negative amount and owes money to the bank. "In the black" means the account shows a positive amount—in other words, there's money in the bank. This comes from the old days of manual accounting, when a negative balance was written in red ink. May you always be in the black!

Another way negative numbers are used is to measure something that is smaller than your standard of measurement. For example, let's say you want to measure the width of an atom, and the only measuring tool you have is a ruler marked off in centimeters. As you know, atoms are so tiny they're not visible to the human eye. You'd have to line up *100 million atoms* side by side just to make *1 centimeter!*

Written as a fraction, the width of one atom would be about 1/100,000,000 of a centimeter. Yikes! That's small! And here we go with all the zeros again. Wait! Remember how exponents can save time and space? Instead of writing 100 million like this:

100,000,000

. . . you can write it like this:

10^8

And 1/100,000,000 is written like this:

10^{-8} or $\dfrac{1}{10^8}$

When working with numbers this small— or even smaller!—people use negative exponents to avoid blisters and headaches.

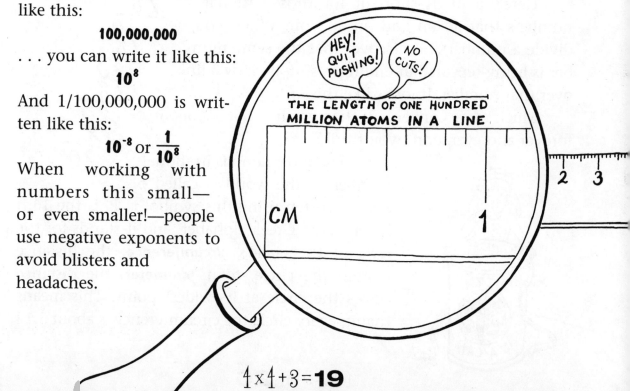

THE LENGTH OF ONE HUNDRED MILLION ATOMS IN A LINE

$4 \times 4 + 3 =$ **19**

Put That Pencil Down—
Irrational Numbers Can't Be Written

Here's a type of number with an odd-sounding name. When a person is described as *irrational*, it means he or she is unreasonable and maybe a little bizarre. **Irrational numbers**, on the other hand, are numbers that are sort of . . . unfinished. For example, let's say you want to know how many times 8 is divisible by 23. The answer is .34782608696 and on and on. This is an example of an irrational number.

There is one big difference between **rational numbers** and irrational numbers. While rational numbers may also go on indefinitely, there is always a pattern to the digits. Take two divided by three, as shown at the right. The sixes literally go on forever, but there is an order to them, thus, it's a rational number.

Here's a math shortcut for those rational numbers that go on and on and on: When you divide a number and discover that the same number is being repeated unendingly, simply draw a line over that number. It looks like this: .$\overline{6}$

Much more convenient than writing .6666666666 forever and ever, don't you think?

The most famous irrational number in the world is called **pi** and is written using this symbol π. Pi is the 16th letter of the Greek alphabet, and it stands for the **ratio** of the circle's **circumference**, the distance around the circle, to its **diameter**, the distance across the circle at its widest point. This means that in every circle the circumference is about 3.14

times longer than its diameter. No exceptions. Guaranteed. Since the number just can't be written in its entirety, the symbol π is a convenient way to refer to this relationship. So, go figure . . . for a few hundred years, that is, because that's how long mathematicians have been dividing out this baby. (And you thought *your* math assignments took forever!)

At last count, pi was calculated to over 6 billion decimal places! It took Daisuke Takahashi and his computers five days to calculate. That was in 1995. If you check *The Guinness Book of World Records* every couple of years, you'll probably see that new people have discovered even more decimal places.

Why all the fascination with pi? It seems to be a mathematical challenge that has held up over time. People want to see how many more decimal places this number has— maybe they want to get into *The*

AWESOME MATH FACTOID

Just as some schools hold spelling bees, others hold contests to see who can memorize π to the most decimal places. The current record holder is Hideaki Tomoyori of Japan, who recited π to 40,000 decimal places! It took him 17 hours!

Guinness Book of World Records, too! All you need to know is an approximation of π to two decimal places, 3.14. But wouldn't it be great if you could recite it to eight decimal places? Can you imagine the look on your math teacher's face? Just memorize this phrase:

Joe, I want a spicy enchilada or tamale lunch.

Just substitute the number of letters in each word for each digit in π. The word "Joe" has three letters, the comma stands for the decimal point, the word "I" has one letter, and so on. It's an easy way to remember π to eight decimal places: 3.14159265.

EXCELLENT equations to *Know & Love*

If you know the diameter (D) or the **radius** (R) of a circle, you can find the circumference (C) by multiplying the diameter by π. Since the radius equals half of the diameter, you can multiply the radius times 2, then multiply by π.

$$D \times \pi = C \text{ or } R \times 2 \times \pi = C$$

Conversely, if you know the circumference of a circle, you can find its diameter or radius by dividing the circumference by π.

$$D = \frac{C}{\pi} \text{ or } 2 \times R = \frac{C}{\pi}, \text{ so } R = \frac{C}{2 \times \pi}$$

How long is a number with a billion decimal places?

To get an idea of how long a number with over 1 billion decimal places really is, let's make some quick calculations. Here is π calculated to 30 decimal places:

3.141592653589793238462643383279

Using a ruler, count how many digits of the number above equal 1 inch. It should be six digits. Divide 1 billion by the number of digits per inch to find the length of π in inches. Ignore any numbers after the decimal point.

1,000,000,000 ÷ 6 = 166,666,666 inches

Divide the number of inches by 12 to find the length of π in feet.

166,666,666 ÷ 12 = 13,888,888 feet

Divide the number of feet by 5,280 to find the length of π in miles.

13,888,888 ÷ 5,280 = 2,630 miles

That's quite a distance! In fact, if this number with a billion decimal places was printed on one line using digits the size shown above, this irrational number would reach from Los Angeles, California, all the way to Washington, D.C.!

Look! A Trapezoid!!

Nobody's Perfect,
But Some Numbers Are

You know how some people are just . . . *sooooooo* *perfect*? Well, numbers can be perfect, too. In this case, being "perfect" has to do with the sum of a number's factors. What's a *factor*? It's simply a number that divides evenly into another number. For example:

1, 3, and 7 are factors of 21.

1, 5, and 7 are factors of 35.

Let's add the factors of 21. Remember, if they add up to 21, it means that 21 is a *perfect number*:

$$1 + 3 + 7 = 11$$

Loser! Not perfect. How about 35?

$$1 + 5 + 7 = 12$$

Double loser! When searching for perfect numbers, don't count the number itself as a factor. In the example above, neither 21 nor 35 should be included in the *equation*. An *equation* is a mathematical statement that contains an equal sign.

What about the number 6? 1, 2, and 3 are factors of 6.

$$1 + 2 + 3 = 6$$

Perfect!

Mathematicians have searched for perfect numbers since the time of Pythagoras. To date, only 32 perfect numbers have been identified. So far, all the perfect numbers are *even* numbers. Is there an *odd* perfect number out there? This is one of the most famous unsolved math mysteries, and mathematicians continue in their quest for perfect numbers, even today.

Only four perfect numbers are smaller than the number 10,000. Perfect numbers start to get very large after 8,128. So large, in fact, that there isn't enough room to list the rest of them here. And the latest perfect number, found in 1992, has 455,663 digits and must be written as a mathematical formula to save space! In case you're wondering, it looks like this:

$$(2^{756,838} - 1) \times 2^{756,838}$$

$$4 \times 6 = \mathbf{24}$$

So you've learned a bit about all different types of numbers—negative and irrational, gigantic and perfect. Now it's time to play with those numbers and see how magical—and cool—math can be!

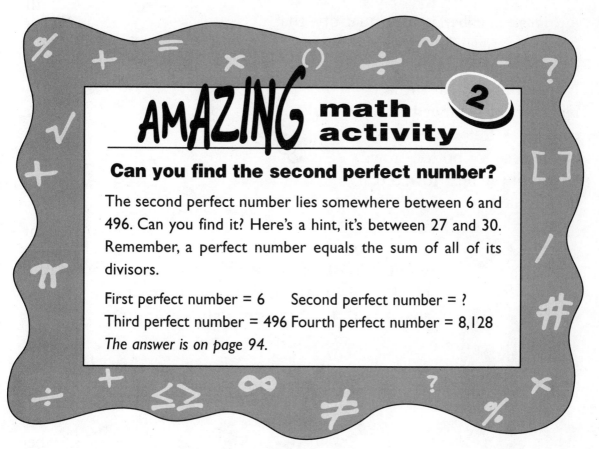

AMAZING math activity ②

Can you find the second perfect number?

The second perfect number lies somewhere between 6 and 496. Can you find it? Here's a hint, it's between 27 and 30. Remember, a perfect number equals the sum of all of its divisors.

First perfect number = 6   Second perfect number = ?
Third perfect number = 496 Fourth perfect number = 8,128
The answer is on page 94.

Totally Buff Numbers!

Like people, certain numbers have shapes. For this next section, instead of seeing numbers as digits (which are only symbols), think of them as objects (marbles, chocolate candies, pistachio nuts, etc.), and try to visualize how the objects look. By

seeing in your mind the amount, you are concentrating on the *quantity* of the number rather than the number itself.

Triangles: Rack 'Em Up

A **triangle number** is any quantity that can be arranged into rows that gradually increase by one. For example, 15 billiard balls can be arranged in a **triangle** as follows: 5 balls at the base, or bottom row; 4 balls in the next row; 3 balls in the next row; 2 in the next

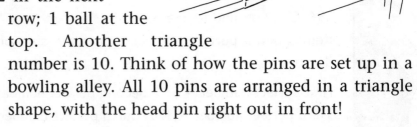

row; 1 ball at the top. Another triangle number is 10. Think of how the pins are set up in a bowling alley. All 10 pins are arranged in a triangle shape, with the head pin right out in front!

Look! An ellipse!

Is the fourth perfect number triangular?

The first three perfect numbers—6, 28, and 496—are also triangle numbers. If you're really motivated, try to figure out if the fourth perfect number is triangular!

AMAZING math activity

③

Can you find the 10 triangular numbers from 1 to 55?

It's easy to find the first few triangular numbers: Simply draw rows of dots that gradually increase by one dot.

But after a while you start to see dots everywhere! Is there another way to find triangular numbers without going absolutely dotty? Well, of course there is.

When you drew those ever-expanding triangles, you added an extra dot to the bottom row. Here's the mathematical sentence that describes what you did when you drew the 10-dot triangle:

$$1 + 2 + 3 + 4 = 10$$

Or, if you look at it another way,

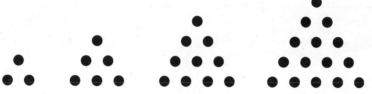

$$\bullet \qquad = 1$$
$$\bullet\bullet \qquad = 1+2$$
$$\bullet\bullet\bullet \qquad = 1+2+3$$
$$\bullet\bullet\bullet\bullet \qquad = 1+2+3+4 \qquad \longrightarrow$$

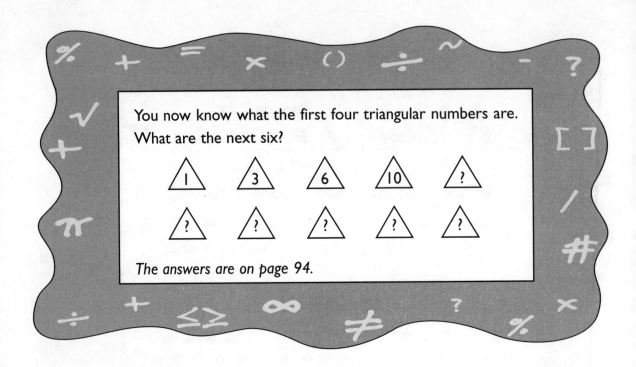

You now know what the first four triangular numbers are. What are the next six?

△ 1   △ 3   △ 6   △ 10   △ ?

△ ?   △ ?   △ ?   △ ?   △ ?

The answers are on page 94.

Squares: Stack 'Em Up

Do you like to play tic-tac-toe? If you do, you're sure to be familiar with the "squareness" of the number nine. A tic-tac-toe board shows three rows of three playing **squares** (3 by 3) for a total of nine playing squares. A **square number** is the result of multiplying a number by itself—in this case, the number three. If you multiply 3 x 3, you get 9 (a square number), the total number of squares in tic-tac-toe.

Remember exponents? Here, 3 x 3 is equal to 3^2, which we call "three to the second power" or "three squared." All numbers with the number two as an exponent mean "squared."

To check the "squareness" of any number, take the same number of objects and line them up in equal rows and columns.

COOL CALCULATIONS

Can you get a square number by adding consecutive integers?

If you add up any number of *consecutive* (one after another) *odd* **integers** (integers are even and odd whole numbers and zero), starting with one, you will always get a square number. For example:

$1 + 3 = 4$ or 2^2
$1 + 3 + 5 = 9$ or 3^2
$1 + 3 + 5 + 7 = 16$ or 4^2
$1 + 3 + 5 + 7 + 9 = 25$ or 5^2
$1 + 3 + 5 + 7 + 9 + 11 = ?$ or __
$1 + 3 + 5 + 7 + 9 + 11 + 13 = ?$ or __
$1 + 3 + 5 + 7 + 9 + 11 + 13 + 15 = ?$ or __
$1 + 3 + 5 + 7 + 9 + 11 + 13 + 15 + 17 = ?$ or __
$1 + 3 + 5 + 7 + 9 + 11 + 13 + 15 + 17 + 19 = ?$ or __

The answers are on page 94.

Look! A Triangle!

NUMBER MAGIC

Here's a grab bag of cool magic tricks you can do to amaze your friends. Everyone will think you're a professional magician when you correctly guess a card chosen by a friend, predict the answers to complex calculations, and even tell someone on what day of the week he or she was born. Each trick is totally dependent on the magic of mathematics!

Get Ready for Sets

A **set** is a group of objects or numbers that are related in some way. A set could be six basketballs, four puppies, odd numbers, even numbers, and so on. If you look around, you can probably find many examples of sets. (How about your 10 fingers?) You also can create sets when you sort objects or numbers into categories you make up on your own.

Objects or numbers that belong in one set also can belong in another. Where two sets come together (or what they have in common) is called the **intersection**. You've probably seen intersections, or **subsets**, illustrated in diagrams like this one:

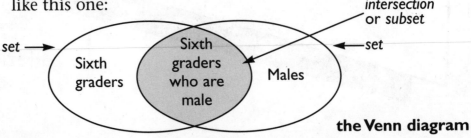

the Venn diagram

90 ÷ 3 = **30**

The **Venn diagram** is named for **John Venn**, a British teacher. He was an ordained Evangelical priest, but left the priesthood at age 49 to teach and study logic full time. He got the idea for the Venn diagram after studying what were then called **Euler circles**, named after **Leonhard Euler** (pronounced "oiler").

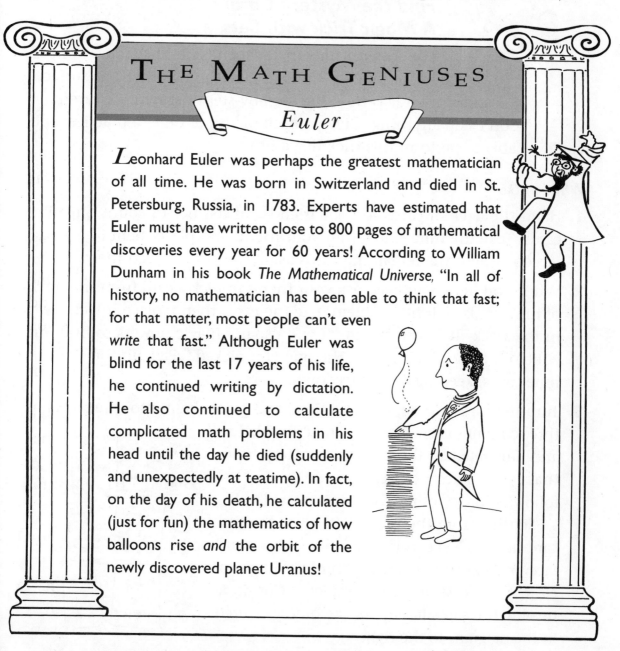

THE MATH GENIUSES

Euler

*L*eonhard Euler was perhaps the greatest mathematician of all time. He was born in Switzerland and died in St. Petersburg, Russia, in 1783. Experts have estimated that Euler must have written close to 800 pages of mathematical discoveries every year for 60 years! According to William Dunham in his book *The Mathematical Universe,* "In all of history, no mathematician has been able to think that fast; for that matter, most people can't even *write* that fast." Although Euler was blind for the last 17 years of his life, he continued writing by dictation. He also continued to calculate complicated math problems in his head until the day he died (suddenly and unexpectedly at teatime). In fact, on the day of his death, he calculated (just for fun) the mathematics of how balloons rise *and* the orbit of the newly discovered planet Uranus!

The intersection of sets is the secret to the following card trick, "Find the Mystery Card," which will surprise your friends and leave them wondering, "How'd you do that?"

Find the Mystery Card: A Magic Trick with Sets

The secret of this trick depends on sets. You will need a deck of playing cards, a tabletop or other flat surface, and a friend. Follow the step-by-step instructions carefully; don't skip anything. Give yourself plenty of time to practice, and you'll be able to perform this trick like a pro!

What to Do:

1. Hand the deck of cards to your friend and tell her to count out nine cards. Take the nine cards from your friend and place them in a stack, facedown. Put the remaining cards aside; you won't need them.

2. While you hide your eyes, ask your friend to pick a card from the stack of nine cards. Tell her to memorize the card, then replace it facedown in the stack. Tell your friend, "I will use my magic powers to find out which of these nine cards is the one you picked." Pick up the stack of nine cards, keeping them facedown.

3. Turn the cards faceup, one at a time, and place them into three rows of three columns each, exactly as described below and illustrated in the diagram. It's important that you place the cards exactly in the following order, otherwise this trick will fail!

Starting from the upper left, place the first card faceup. Next to it, place the second card faceup. Next to it, place the third card faceup. Now your first row is complete. Continue turning the cards faceup, in the order pictured in the diagram to the right.

Row 1

Row 2

Row 3

100−68=**32**

4. Say to your friend, "Without telling me which card is yours, point to the *row* your card is in." The *row* she points to tells you which *column* her card will be in the next time you lay the cards out (in step 6).

- If she points to the first row, her card will be in the first column.
- If she points to the second row, her card will be in the second column.
- If she points to the third row, her card will be in the third column.

Let's say she chose the eight of clubs, which is in the second row. It will appear in the second column next time.

5. Now, pick up the cards *in the exact same order* you laid them down. To do this, pick up the first card you laid down. Hold it faceup in your hand. Pick up the second card you laid down and place it faceup under the first card. Pick up the third card and place it faceup under the other cards. Do the same for the remaining cards, one card at a time.

6. Hold the stack of cards in your hand, faceup. You will lay them out in a square again, but there's a big difference in the way you'll do it this time.

Instead of laying the cards across in rows, you'll place them in columns going down: Starting from the upper left, place the first card faceup. Place the second card below the first card. Place the third card below the second card. Start a new column, continuing to place the cards faceup, in their order on the diagram.

7. Say to your friend, "Point to the row your card is in." When she does, you'll find her card at the exact spot where that row and the second column *intersect!* In the example above, her card is in the third row. The third row and second column intersect at the eight of clubs. Pause dramatically, close your eyes, touch your temples, and announce, "Your card is the eight of clubs!"

$$99 \div 3 = \mathbf{33}$$

Why It Works: As we said before, a set is any collection of objects or numbers. In this case, the sets were rows of cards and columns of cards. Each row of cards was a set. Each column of cards was a set.

In the first pattern you laid out, you found out which row held the secret card. This information also immediately pointed to which column the card belonged to (see step 4). In this case, the secret card belonged to the Row 2 set, which became the Column 2 set the next time the cards were laid out. The next step was simply to lay the cards out again, this time in columns, and find out which row the card was in. In this trick, the card was in Row 3. So, when you took Column 2 (which you figured from the first pattern) and Row 3 from the second pattern, the intersecting card is the eight of clubs. You revealed the secret identity of the card.

This trick is described using nine cards, but it's even more amazing to use more cards. How many more? As long as you make sure all the cards form a square, there's no limit to the amount. The square numbers you can use with one deck of cards are 9 (3 rows of 3), 16 (4 rows of 4), 25 (5 rows of 5), 36 (6 rows of 6), or 49 (7 rows of 7). Your friends will be astounded when they see how your magic powers allow you to predict the exact position of a single card, even in a group of 49 cards!

Playing It Cool with Number Patterns

A ***pattern*** is a group of something, in this case numbers, that are related in a predictable way. Look at this list of numbers:

$$2, \quad 4, \quad 6, \quad 8, \quad 10, \quad 12, \ldots$$

Can you predict what number will come next in this pattern? Sure, 14! By adding 2 to each number, we get the next number in the pattern.

Patterns are important because they help mathematicians solve complicated math problems. Often a pattern will reveal a shortcut to solving the problem. Read on for some amazing patterns that can help you check your arithmetic and surprise your friends.

AMAZING math activity

4

Take a friend's favorite number and produce it again and again and again and again. . . .

1. Ask a friend what his favorite number is between one and nine. (It must be a single-digit number.)

2. In your head, multiply the number by nine and write the answer underneath your magic "favorite number generator": 12,345,679.

It's easy to remember this number—it's simply consecutive numbers one through nine *without the eight.*

For example, let's say your friend tells you his favorite number is two. Write the number 18 (2 x 9) underneath 12,345,679 so it looks like this:

12,345,679

x 18

Now ask your friend to do the multiplication problem. Look at the answer: **222,222,222**! His favorite digit has grown! This works with every number between one and nine.

Nine: A Pattern Powerhouse

There are so many cool patterns to make with the number nine, we could fill a book with them! It's no surprise that ancient Greeks considered the number nine to be the symbol for indestructibility. Why? Because nine always comes back to itself. Sounds mysterious, doesn't it? Read on.

Multiples of Nine Always Add Up to Nine

Take a look at the pattern in the nine-times multiplication table:

9 x 1 = 9	
9 x 2 = 18	1 + 8 = 9
9 x 3 = 27	2 + 7 = 9
9 x 4 = 36	3 + 6 = 9
9 x 5 = 45	4 + 5 = 9
9 x 6 = 54	5 + 4 = 9
9 x 7 = 63	6 + 3 = 9
9 x 8 = 72	7 + 2 = 9
9 x 9 = 81	8 + 1 = 9
9 x 10 = 90	9 + 0 = 9

Did you notice that once you got to 9 x 6, the answers were simply *transposed* versions (both digits were reversed) of earlier **products**? A product is the answer you get when you multiply two or more numbers together. Also, whenever you multiply nine by another number—*any* other number—the sum of the digits in the answer always adds up to nine or another number whose digits added together equal nine.

Such as:　　9 x 347 = 3,123　　　　　　　3 + 1 + 2 + 3 = 9

　　　　　　　9 x 568 = 5,112　　　　　　　5 + 1 + 1 + 2 = 9

Sometimes you have to add the digits twice before reaching nine.

　　　　　9 x 22 = 198　　　1 + 9 + 8 = 18　　　1 + 8 = 9

　　　　　9 x 762 = 6,858　　6 + 8 + 5 + 8 = 27　　2 + 7 = 9

Here's another pattern using multiples of nine:

a. 9 x 0 + 1 = 1

b. 9 x 1 + 2 = 11

c. 9 x 12 + 3 = 111

d. 9 x 123 + 4 = 1,111

e. 9 x 1234 + 5 =

f. 9 x 12345 + 6 =

g. 9 x 123456 + 7 =

h. 9 x 1234567 + 8 =

Did you spot the pattern? What do you think the answers are for equations "e" through "h"? If you have a calculator handy, solve the problems and see if you guessed right. If you don't have a calculator, grab a pencil and a sheet of paper and figure it out. *The answers are on page 94.*

Here is a pattern involving the number nine and its neighbor, eight.

9 x 9 + 7 = 88

9 x 98 + 6 = 888

9 x 987 + 5 = 8,888

9 x 9876 + 4 = 88,888

9 x 98765 + 3 = 888,888

9 x 987654 + 2 = 8,888,888

9 x 9876543 + 1 = 88,888,888

Note to Reader: You must always skip one number before adding the single digit.

AMAZING math activity

5

Number Nine Every Time!

Here's a fun number magic trick that always contains the number nine. Try it on a friend! Follow these instructions exactly.

1. Say to your friend, "Think of a long number that you know by heart. It could be a phone number, a ZIP code, even a birthdate. When you've thought of the number, don't tell me what it is. Write it down on a piece of paper and don't let me see it." Let's say your friend writes the number 913305.

6913305

2. Next, tell your friend, "You may rearrange the digits in the number any way you like: backward or just scrambled any old way." Let's say your friend writes 5033196.

5033196

3. Next, say, "Please subtract the smaller number from the bigger one." In this case, your friend will subtract 5033196 from 6913305.

```
  6913305
- 5033196
  1880109
```

→

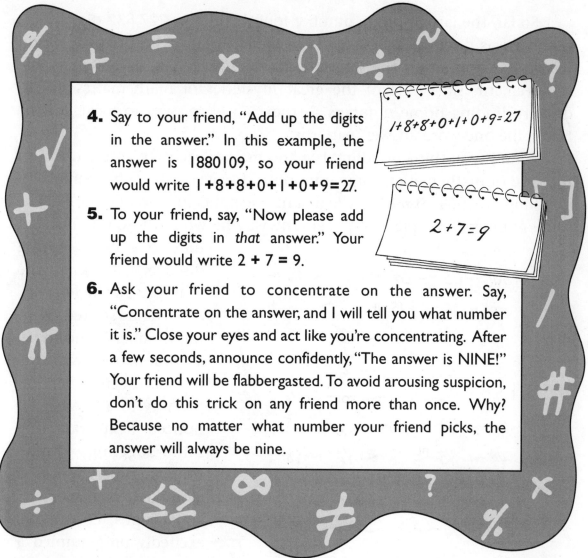

4. Say to your friend, "Add up the digits in the answer." In this example, the answer is 1880109, so your friend would write 1+8+8+0+1+0+9=27.

$1+8+8+0+1+0+9=27$

5. To your friend, say, "Now please add up the digits in *that* answer." Your friend would write 2 + 7 = 9.

$2+7=9$

6. Ask your friend to concentrate on the answer. Say, "Concentrate on the answer, and I will tell you what number it is." Close your eyes and act like you're concentrating. After a few seconds, announce confidently, "The answer is NINE!" Your friend will be flabbergasted. To avoid arousing suspicion, don't do this trick on any friend more than once. Why? Because no matter what number your friend picks, the answer will always be nine.

Doodles and Discoveries:
Finding a Pattern in Prime Numbers

A **prime number** is a number that can be divided only by the number one and itself. Here are some examples of prime numbers:

 2   3   5   7   11   13

(By the way, the number two is the only *even* prime number.)

13 x 3 = 39

So far, the largest prime number found contains 227,832 digits. This number was discovered by experts in Great Britain who hold the world record for computing the largest prime number. This is a remarkable achievement, since one of the great mysteries of mathematics has to do with finding prime numbers. Is there an easier way to locate them? Here's the one-word answer: patterns.

Now, if you think doodling is a "no-brainer" activity, think again! In the field of mathematics, some important discoveries have been made by doodling. In 1964, **Stanislaw Ulam**, a mathematician (and doodler), wrote some numbers on a piece of paper. The way he wrote those numbers led him to a very exciting discovery. Look at the examples to the left.

Ulam started with the number 1 and made a spiral pattern with the rest of the numbers all the way to 49. What he noticed next was truly mind-boggling: Many prime numbers appeared along diagonal lines!

Ulam's co-workers excitedly programmed a computer, called the "Maniac II," to create the spiral pattern of numbers on a much larger scale. To their amazement, the same thing happened. Many prime numbers fell along diagonal lines.

```
37 — 36 — 35 — 34 — 33 — 32 — 31
38   17 — 16 — 15 — 14 — 13   30
39   18    5 — 4 — 3    12   29
40   19    6   1 — 2   11   28
41   20    7 — 8 — 9 — 10   27
42   21 — 22 — 23 — 24 — 25 — 26
43 — 44 — 45 — 46 — 47 — 48 — 49
```

Ulam's doodle

```
[37] — 36 — 35 — 34 — 33 — 32 — [31]
38   [17] — 16 — 15 — 14 — [13]   30
39   18   [5] — 4 — [3]   12   [29]
40   [19]   6   1 — [2]   [11]   28
[41]   20   [7] — 8 — 9 — 10   27
42   21 — 22 — [23] — 24 — 25 — 26
[43] — 44 — 45 — 46 — [47] — 48 — 49
```

AMAZING math activity

6

Filter numbers through Eratosthenes' Sieve to reveal all the primes from 1 to 100.

Eratosthenes (ehr-uh-TAHS-thuh-neez) was a Greek astronomer and geographer. In 200 B.C.E., he invented this classic method for finding prime numbers, and it's still one of the best.

1. On graph paper, make a chart of the numbers from 1 to 100, with 10 numbers in each row.

2. Cross out the number 1: It is not prime.

3. Leave the number 2: It is prime. Cross out all multiples of 2: They are not prime since they can be divided by 2. (This eliminates all the even numbers.)

4. Leave the number 3: It is prime. Cross out all multiples of 3 (every third number).

5. Leave the number 5: It is prime. Cross out all multiples of 5, that is, every number that can be divided by 5.

6. Leave the number 7: It is prime. Cross out all multiples of 7.

7. Leave the number 11: It is prime. Cross out all multiples of 11.

8. Your chart shows all the prime numbers through 100; all the rest have passed through Eratosthenes' Sieve.

The answer is on page 94.

These mathematicians had discovered a brand-new way to find prime numbers. All it took was a little doodling and a big Maniac. Doodle on, kids of the world—you never know what secrets can be found in an innocent little scribble!

Sequences Let You Predict the Future or Unlock the Past!

A ***sequence*** is a set of numbers that come one after another arranged in a certain order. A sequence has a pattern of its own, but this pattern has a particular order. You might say that a sequence has a pattern within a pattern, or a pattern of patterns. Because of this order, sequences are predictable and allow you to ***extrapolate***, which means to figure what comes before or what will come after the sequence.

COOL CALCULATIONS

On Which Day of the Week Were You Born?

The days and months of a calendar are a sequence. You know the date on which you were born, but do you know on which day of the week you were born? What about the day of the week on which your younger sibling or cousin was born? You can figure it out by extrapolating. Below, the months of the year and the days of the week have been assigned numbers to help you find the answer.

Months

January	1*	July	0
February	4*	August	3
March	4	September	6
April	0	October	1
May	2	November	4
June	5	December	6

Days

Sunday	1
Monday	2
Tuesday	3
Wednesday	4
Thursday	5
Friday	6
Saturday	0

*(*For leap years—1976, 1980, 1984, 1988, 1992, 1996, and 2000—change January to 0 and February to 3.)*

Okay, let's begin with a test date. Let's say you were born on August 9, 1983.

1. Write down the last two digits of the year you were born.

83

2. Divide the number by four. Ignore any **remainder** (any number left over, beyond the whole number).

83 ÷ 4 = 20, remainder 3. Answer: 20

3. Look at the chart of months on the previous page, and find the digit that represents your month.

3

4. Now write down the date on which you were born.

9

5. You now have four numbers. Add them all together.

83 + 20 + 3 + 9 = 115

6. Divide this number by seven. The remainder is the number that is equal to the day on which you were born. If there isn't a remainder, you were born on a Saturday.

115 ÷ 7 = 16, remainder 3

Look up "3" on the chart of days. You were born on a Tuesday.

Look! A 4-sided polygon, or a quadrilateral, or a square!

AMAZING math activity

7

Can you calculate the sum of all nine numbers circled on this calendar— in just one second?

Su	M	Tu	W	Th	F	Sa
			1	2	3	4
5	6	7	8	9	10	11
12	13	14	15	16	17	18
19	20	21	22	23	24	25
26	27	28	29	30		

Here's the secret (but first, put down your pencil):

1. Multiply the number in the very center of the group (9) by 9. If you've memorized your multiplication facts, you'll know in a heartbeat that the answer is 81!

2. Now take out your pencil or a calculator and add up all nine numbers. What's the sum?

3. Try this trick with other nine-number groups on a calendar page. Just remember that you must group the numbers in 3 x 3 boxes, exactly as shown here. (The secret to this trick lies in the consecutive order of the numbers.)

HIGH-TECH WORLD, LOW-TECH NUMBERS

Computers, Web sites, digital sound, CDs, and CD-ROM games are possible because of two very low-tech numbers. What are they? The numbers zero and one. That's it.

Binary Numbers: A Mighty Pair

Look at the following words and see if you can spot what they have in common:

bicycle

binoculars

bilingual

/00/0/0///0/

binary

All the words above start with *bi-*, which means two. A bicycle has two wheels, binoculars have two lenses, someone who is bilingual speaks two languages, and **binary** is simply a number system that uses two numbers: zero and one. Would you believe that you can combine these two numbers to make any number you like? You can. The secret lies in place value.

Counting Systems Around the World

The San people of Africa, one of the oldest African cultures, use a binary counting system. This is how they count to 10:

San binary number system	Base 10 number system
One	= 1
One pair	= 2
One pair and one	= 3
Two pairs	= 4
Two pairs and one	= 5
Three pairs	= 6
Three pairs and one	= 7
Four pairs	= 8
Four pairs and one	= 9
Five pairs	= 10

Other tribal peoples such as the Zamuco Indians of South America, the Kauralgal people of Australia, and the Parb people of New Guinea also use a binary counting system. What do all these people have in common besides their counting system? The answer is: Their cultures are very, very, very old. Some scholars suggest that the binary counting system was the first counting system of most cultures throughout the world. As life changed, so did the counting systems, except in certain isolated groups of people whose way of life hasn't changed much over the centuries. (As you'll soon learn, the binary counting system has made a smashing, world-wide comeback in the 20th century with the development of computers.)

As some early societies grew larger and became more complex, so did their counting systems. Certain cultures found they could get along just fine with a *base two number system*. Others developed different number systems: For example, the Mayan Indians used a *base five counting system*—called a **vigesimal system**. Our counting system, the base 10 number system, is based on the number 10. All our place values are in powers of 10.

Look at this number: **524**

✔ The first number is in the hundreds column and is a 5. It stands for 5 hundreds.

✔ The next number is in the tens column, so we know it stands for 2 tens.

✔ The last number is in the ones column, so we know it stands for 4 ones.

Now do a little addition: **500 + 20 + 4 = 524**.

Thousands	Hundreds	Tens	Ones
0	**500**	**20**	**4**

In the binary system, 524 would be 100000110, because the place values are different. There is a place value for ones (1), a place value for twos (2 x 1), fours (2 x 2), eights (2 x 2 x 2), sixteens (2 x 2 x 2 x 2), thirty-twos (2 x 2 x 2 x 2 x 2), sixty-fours (2 x 2 x 2 x 2 x 2 x 2), and so on. So, 524 would be separated like:

512	256	128	64	32	16	8	4	2	1
1	**0**	**0**	**0**	**0**	**0**	**1**	**1**	**0**	**0**

Look at this binary number. It looks like one hundred and one, but it's not! Remember, we're using the binary system.

101
fours twos ones

✔ The first number, 1, is in the fours column, and it stands for 1 four.

✔ The next number, 0, is in the twos column, and it stands for 0 twos.

✔ The next number, 1, is in the ones column, and it stands for 1 one. Now do a little addition: **4 + 0 + 1 = 5**. This binary number equals what we call "five" in our base 10 number system.

Let's try translating the binary number 111.

✔ The first number, 1, is in the fours column, so we know it stands for 1 four.

✔ The next number, 1, is in the twos column, so we know it stands for 1 two.

✔ The next number, 1, is in the ones column, so we know it stands for 1 one.

Here's the addition: **4 + 2 + 1 = 7**.

This is what the numbers 1 through 10 look like as binary numbers:

Binary numbers					Calculations		Base 10 numbers
8	4	2	1				
			1	=			1
		1	0	=	2 + 0	=	2
		1	1	=	2 + 1	=	3
	1	0	0	=	4 + 0 + 0	=	4
	1	0	1	=	4 + 0 + 1	=	5
	1	1	0	=	4 + 2 + 0	=	6
	1	1	1	=	4 + 2 + 1	=	7
1	0	0	0	=	8 + 0 + 0 + 0	=	8
1	0	0	1	=	8 + 0 + 0 + 1	=	9
1	0	1	0	=	8 + 0 + 2 + 0	=	10

As you can see, this system is very simple because it uses only two digits, but the combinations of those digits tend to get very long very quickly. For example, the binary number for 32 looks like this: 100000.

The binary system as we know it today was invented in the late 1600s by a German-born mathematician, **Gottfried Wilhelm Leibniz**. No one got too excited about binary numbers back then because they looked so weird. Who wanted to work with such strange-looking long numbers? The world waited 300 years for an answer, and the answer was: computer programmers!

Programmers realized that computers would be able to understand binary numbers perfectly. Why? Computers are powered by electricity and can understand only two values: "on" or "off." Programmers realized they could translate these values into numbers: "On" would be the number one and "off" would be zero. The programmers could "talk" to computers by using binary numbers. This was the beginning of the computer age!

When you give a computer a binary number like 10010, the computer thinks of it this way: ON OFF OFF ON OFF. Here is how a computer understands the numbers one through five in binary.

Binary		Computer	Base 10 number system
1	=	ON	1
10	=	ON OFF	2
11	=	ON ON	3
100	=	ON OFF OFF	4
101	=	ON OFF ON	5

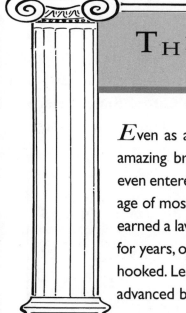

THE MATH GENIUSES

Leibniz

*E*ven as a child, Gottfried Wilhelm Leibniz showed amazing brainpower. He learned things quickly, and even entered college when he was 15 years old—the age of most high-school freshmen! Although Leibniz earned a law degree and worked as a legal consultant for years, once he began studying mathematics he was hooked. Leibniz is best known for the creation of an advanced branch of mathematics, called *calculus*.

LEIBNIZ

Bamboozle Your Buddies with Binary Boxes!

Everyone will think you're a mind reader when you perform this astounding trick. You'll even amaze yourself when you try it alone. Be sure to follow all the instructions exactly. Before trying it on a friend, practice several times on your own.

First, get five 3" x 5" cards and five small markers, such as pennies or jellybeans. Then copy the rows of numbers listed on the next page onto the cards exactly the way you see them printed.

$7^2 = $ **49**

What to Do:

1. Tell your friend to pick a number from one of the cards. Don't let him tell you what the number is.

2. Ask your friend which cards the number appears on. Place a marker on each of those cards.

3. Okay, here comes the good part! Now look at all the cards that have markers on them. Add up the numbers in the top left corner of each card. For example, if there are markers on Card 2 and Card 4, add the first number from Card 2 (binary place value of 2) and the first number from Card 4 (binary place value of 8) and you get 10. Loudly announce that your friend picked the number . . . 10! Ta daaaa! Smile nicely while everyone claps and whistles in amazement at your powers of ESP!

1	3	5	7
9	11	13	15
17	19	21	23
25	27	29	31

Card 1

2	3	6	7
10	11	14	15
18	19	22	23
26	27	30	31

Card 2

4	5	6	7
12	13	14	15
20	21	22	23
28	29	30	31

Card 3

8	9	10	11
12	13	14	15
24	25	26	27
28	29	30	31

Card 4

16	17	18	19
20	21	22	23
24	25	26	27
28	29	30	31

Card 5

Why It Works: Each card stands for a binary place value. Cards 1, 2, 3, 4, and 5 match the binary place values of 1, 2, 4, 8, 16. The numbers that appear on the cards all have a "1" in that place value column. For example, all the numbers on Card 2 have a "1" in the "twos" column of a binary number. When you add the numbers in the top left corner of the two marked cards, you get the only number that has a "1" in both the "twos" column and the "eights" column.

More Binary Magic

Sort a deck of playing cards by value (all the kings together, the queens together, etc.) —without looking! Even the brainiest won't be able to figure out how you, the amazing math magician, can do *this* cool card trick. Follow the step-by-step instructions and take your time. It's important to go slowly in the beginning, when you're just learning the trick. Later you can pick up speed and really dazzle your audience.

What to Do:

1. Find a complete set of playing cards. Take out the jokers and set them aside.

2. Take a look at the number table on the next page. At first, keep it close by as you perform this trick; you'll probably need to refer to it. The table shows all the cards written as binary numbers. The face cards, the Jack, Queen, and King, have been given the values of 11, 12, and 13, respectively.

Card	Binary Place Value			
	8	**4**	**2**	**1**
Ace				1
Two			1	0
Three			1	1
Four		1	0	0
Five		1	0	1
Six		1	1	0
Seven		1	1	1
Eight	1	0	0	0
Nine	1	0	0	1
Ten	1	0	1	0
Jack	1	0	1	1
Queen	1	1	0	0
King	1	1	0	1

3. Turn the deck over so the cards are faceup, toward you, just like in the illustration.

4. Start to sort the cards into two piles, one on the right and one on the left. The pile on the left will hold all your discards. The first cards you will look for are the cards that have a "1" in the ones column. They are: ➤

Go through the deck of cards in your hand, one card at a time. Every time you find one of the cards to the right, place it facedown on the pile on your right. Place the other cards facedown on the pile on your left.

5. When you've gone through all the cards, place the pile of cards on the right facedown on top of the cards on the left.

6. Turn the deck over so all the cards are facing up, just like before. Now you will start to sort for the twos, which are:

Go through the cards one at a time. Every time you find one of the cards to the right, place it facedown on the pile on your right. Place the other cards facedown on the pile on your left.

7. When you've gone through all the cards, place the pile of cards on the right facedown on top of the cards on the left.

8. Turn the deck over so all the cards are faceup. Now you will start to sort for the fours, which are: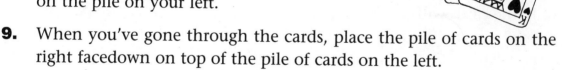

Go through the cards one at a time. Every time you find one of the cards to the right, place it facedown on the pile on your right. Place the other cards facedown on the pile on your left.

9. When you've gone through the cards, place the pile of cards on the right facedown on top of the pile of cards on the left.

10. Turn the deck over so all the cards are faceup. Now you will start to sort for the eights, which are:

Go through the cards one at a time. Every time you find one of the cards to the right, place it facedown on the pile on your right. Place the other cards facedown on the pile on your left.

11. When you've gone through all the cards, place the pile of cards on the right on top of the pile of cards on the left. *And now for the big finish!*

12. Turn the deck over so all the cards are faceup. Go through them one by one. The cards are sorted by their value!

Why It Works: Again, the magic lies in the beauty of the binary system. We translated the cards into binary numbers in the table you saw earlier. As you sorted for each place value, you divided the cards into groups that either had that place value or didn't. When you resorted for the next place value, the higher cards kept getting resorted, so that finally, only the cards with the highest place value (8) went into the pile on the right. That's math magic for you!

CHAPTER 4

Shhhh! Secrets and Spies: Curious Codes and Ciphers

People have passed secret messages back and forth for the last 3,000 years. Writing messages using secret codes is called **cryptography**, a word that comes from the Greek words "kryptos," meaning *secret*, and "graphos," meaning *writing*.

Curious Codes and Ciphers

A **code** uses substitute words, numbers, or symbols in place of each *word* in the secret message. A **cipher** uses numbers or symbols for every *letter* in the secret message. Cracking a code or cipher is a lot like solving a math problem and requires the very same type of skills. In fact, during World War II, expert code-breakers were often math whizzes.

One of the earliest examples of secret writing was used by a famous Greek historian named **Polybius** (puh-LIH-bee-uhs). Polybius was captured during the Roman conquest of Greece, about 168 B.C.E. He made up a cipher to send secret messages.

An Oldie but Goodie: Polybius' 5 x 5 Cipher Square

horizontal number

	1	2	3	4	5
1	A	B	C	D	E
2	F	G	H	I	J
3	K	L	M	N	O
4	P	Q	R	S	T
5	U	V	W	X	Y/Z

vertical number

To write a message using this code, simply write the two numbers that intersect at the letter you want. First write the vertical number, then the horizontal number. For example, **51 = U**.

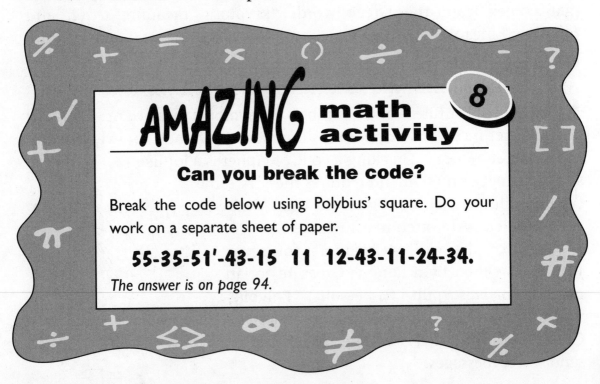

AMAZING math activity

8

Can you break the code?

Break the code below using Polybius' square. Do your work on a separate sheet of paper.

55-35-51'-43-15 11 12-43-11-24-34.

The answer is on page 94.

You probably noticed that Polybius' square is made up of two sets, almost like the sets in the "Find the Mystery Card" trick on page 32. The rows are one set, the columns are another set. Both sets intersect at the coded letter.

If you want to send or translate messages with a friend using Polybius' square, you have to re-create the square on a piece of paper. This is called a **key**, because it shows how the code works. (Be careful not to let the key fall into the wrong hands, or your secret message won't be so secret anymore.)

Caesar's Shift Cipher

The Roman Emperor *Julius Caesar* invented a cipher called the "Caesar Shift" (not to be confused with the Caesar Salad, which is quite delicious but crummy for sending messages). This cipher gives a number to each letter of the alphabet by shifting the alphabet three places to the right. For example, instead of replacing the first letter of the alphabet, *a*, with the number 1 (which is too obvious), you make *a* the number 3.

11 18-20-7-8-7-20
3-16-5-10-17-24-11-
7-21 17-16 15-27
. 5-3-7-21-3-20'

A	B	C	D	E	F	G	H	I	J	K	L	M
3	4	5	6	7	8	9	10	11	12	13	14	15

N	O	P	Q	R	S	T	U	V	W	X	Y	Z
16	17	18	19	20	21	22	23	24	25	26	27	28

With Caesar's cipher, the secret message below looks like this:

25-10-3-22'-21 23-18, 5-3-7-21-3-20?

(You have 5 seconds to decode this message before it self-destructs. Okay, just kidding. *The answer is on page 94.*)

Beale's Buried Treasure

Over time, ciphers became more complicated. During the 19th century, one of the most fascinating events in the history of cryptography took place. In his book *Archimedes' Revenge,* author Paul Hoffman describes the true story of an adventurer named Thomas Jefferson Beale who appeared in Lynchburg, Virginia, seemingly out of nowhere (he never revealed where he had come from or even if he had any family). After spending a few months in town, Beale disappeared for two years. He returned for a short time and left an iron box with a trusted friend before leaving again. Beale told the friend that the box was not to be opened until 10 years had passed without his return.

The decade passed with no sign of Beale. The box was opened and inside it were papers that described a spectacular buried treasure—tons of gold, silver, and sparkling jewels—and directions on where to find it. However, the directions were nothing but three pages of numbers! (These numbers are printed in their entirety in Paul Hoffman's book, just in case anyone else wants to take a crack at them.) Beale had obviously used a cipher, but where was the key? Beale was never seen or heard from again, and the friend to whom he had entrusted the box died 41 years later. Just before he died, the friend told another man, James Ward, of his inability to decode the message.

Years later, Ward was able to decipher one of the pages because he discovered what Thomas Jefferson Beale had used for a cipher key: the Declaration of Independence! Ward had tried using many other documents before finding the answer in this one.

Declaration of Independence

$\overset{1}{\text{When}}$ $\overset{2}{\text{in}}$ $\overset{3}{\text{the}}$ $\overset{4}{\text{course}}$ $\overset{5}{\text{of}}$ $\overset{6}{\text{human}}$ $\overset{7}{\text{events}}$ $\overset{8}{\text{it}}$ $\overset{9}{\text{becomes}}$ $\overset{10}{\text{necessary}}$ $\overset{11}{\text{for}}$

By numbering each word of the Declaration of Independence, Ward hit upon the solution and was able to decipher the entire page. However, this particular page told only that the treasure consisted of thousands of pounds of gold and silver and millions of dollars' worth of jewels—not where it was buried. (That information was on one of the pages that could not be decoded.)

Cryptographers have been trying for over 170 years, without success, to decipher the other pages or find the millions of dollars' worth of treasure. Some people started a secret club devoted to cracking the code. Even today, using modern computers, the cipher remains a mystery! Will it ever be solved?

Japan's Purple Machine and Other Hard-to-Break Codes

In wartime, it's very important to gather intelligence—just a dramatic word for *information*—about the enemy. Intelligence can be anything from records of military personnel or the location of troops to plans for a top-secret attack. *Intelligence experts* are the people who collect this information. Some of them are spies, and some of them are fantastic code busters. During World War II, some were topnotch math minds handpicked from mathematics programs in Poland and Great Britain.

During World War II, Japan used a cipher machine that U.S. intelligence experts called the "Purple Machine." Based on the Japanese messages they intercepted, U.S. cryptographers were able to build their own version of the machine. With their Purple Machine impostor, the code breakers deciphered incredibly important messages about the location of enemy forces, their plans to attack, and the top-secret schedule of a Japanese admiral.

Another especially complicated code used during World War II was the Nazis' code, called "Enigma," which is a word for something that is mysterious and hard to explain.

The Germans used the Enigma code to communicate with their submarine wolf packs, which attacked ships full of supplies and bound for Great Britain. The wolf packs, gangs of German U-boats, or submarines, operated according to radioed orders from the German navy. Since the orders were sent using the Enigma code, the Allies had no idea how to decipher them.

This cipher was eventually broken by British intelligence experts (one of whom was the famous mathematician *Alan Turing*), and the decoded information helped the Allied forces hunt down and destroy the German submarines in the Battle of the Atlantic, which lasted from 1939 to 1943.

Why Cryptographers Like Prime Numbers

Because prime numbers are so hard to locate, especially when the numbers are very large, they are valuable to cryptographers. Prime numbers make secret computer codes incredibly difficult and time-consuming for outsiders to crack. In fact, the cryptographers who encode national secrets use primes to come up with huge numbers for coding such sensitive material.

In 1977, a group of cryptographers challenged other cryptographers to find the key to their brand-new code. The only way to do it was to find the prime factors of a certain number that was a whopping 129 digits long! At that time, the cryptographers who invented the new code figured it would take about 40 quadrillion (40×10^{15}) years for others to solve the puzzle and crack the code.

This problem was solved in the spring of 1994 in a time span of just *eight months* by 160 computers working together via the Internet on a solution.

THE MATH GENIUSES

Turing

*E*nglishman Alan Turing was a young math scholar when he went to work as a code breaker for the Government Code and Cypher (British spelling for "cipher") School at the onset of the Second World War. There he met other young mathematicians working on the Enigma code. (At this time, secret messages were being encoded using cipher machines, and mathematicians were found to be good **cryptanalysts,** or *decoders,* because they understood how to analyze, or study, problems logically.) Turing is best known for the concept of the "Turing machine," which was the great-granddaddy of today's electronic computers. In 1946 he helped design a digital computer called "ACE," for Automatic Computing Engine. Turing was something of an *eccentric,* which means he was a guy with a lot of quirks. For example, he loved to run. In fact, he was an Olympic-class long-distance runner, but since his wristwatch didn't always work, he ran with an alarm clock tied to a piece of rope.

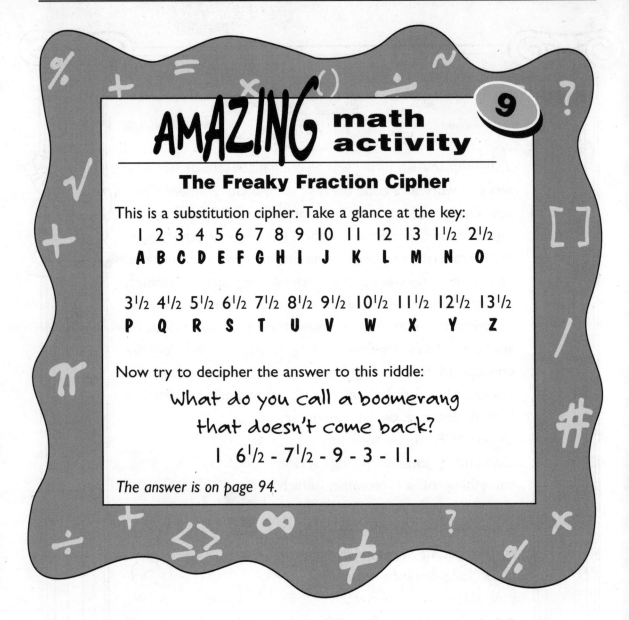

AMAZING math activity

9

The Freaky Fraction Cipher

This is a substitution cipher. Take a glance at the key:

1	2	3	4	5	6	7	8	9	10	11	12	13	1½	2½
A	B	C	D	E	F	G	H	I	J	K	L	M	N	O

3½	4½	5½	6½	7½	8½	9½	10½	11½	12½	13½
P	Q	R	S	T	U	V	W	X	Y	Z

Now try to decipher the answer to this riddle:

What do you call a boomerang that doesn't come back?

1 6½ - 7½ - 9 - 3 - 11.

The answer is on page 94.

THE WILD SIDE OF MATHEMATICS: NUMBERS IN NATURE

Get ready for a walk on the wild side of mathematics—that is, finding numbers in nature. To find the zillions of numbers inhabiting the natural world, you need to take a close look around you. Imagine yourself wearing special glasses that let you focus in on the shapes, patterns, and sequences of natural objects such as leaves, spider webs, or snail shells.

Spirals in Nature

When you look at a pine cone, what do you see? There's one word to describe what makes a pine cone so fascinating to mathematicians: *spirals*. Spirals are beautiful, natural models of a mathematical idea called *exponential growth*. When something grows or increases exponentially, it means it undergoes an extremely rapid increase.

If we turn a pine cone on one end, we can see how the scales form in a spiral. Can you see the spirals? It's not easy if you don't have a practiced eye. Turn to page 65 to see how to find spirals and Fibonacci numbers in pine cones! The Cool Calculations exercise on the next page helps to illustrate exponential growth.

a pine cone—bottoms up!

$9 \times 7 =$ **63**

Look! An Octagon!

COOL CALCULATIONS

If someone gave you a penny and said she would double your money every day, how long do you think it would take for you to become a millionaire?

Answer: Twenty-seven days, or less than one month. Don't believe it? Do the math. Your money would grow "exponentially" to the power of 2 every time it was doubled. Now you know why we said exponential growth is a speeded-up rate of growth. The numbers become very large very quickly. Turn to page 94 to see each math equation!

How does exponential growth in the formation of a pine cone result in a spiral? First of all, everything in the universe moves naturally in spirals, not straight lines—water going down the drain, the way you developed from a tiny embryo, the way hair grows on your head, how planets in our solar system orbit the sun, and even the Milky Way galaxy. So in this swirling, whirling universe, why would spirals on a pine cone be of any interest to you, math whiz extraordinaire? The numbers, babe, the numbers.

Fibonacci Numbers

A **Fibonacci** (Fih-buh-NAH-chee) *sequence* is a pattern of numbers; such patterns are often found in nature. They were made famous by a man named **Leonardo Fibonacci**. In 1202, Fibonacci used this sequence of numbers in a brainteaser he created. It's an easy-to-understand sequence. See if you can spot the pattern:

0	3 + 5 = 8
1	5 + 8 = 13
1 + 1 = 2	8 + 13 = 21
1 + 2 = 3	13 + 21 = 34
2 + 3 = 5	21 + 34 = 55

Just add the last two numbers of the sequence together to get the next number. This is called the **pattern of consecutive sums**.

Here is a list of the first 20 Fibonacci numbers:

0, 1, 1, 2, 3, 5, 8, 13, 21, 34, 55, 89, 144, 233, 377, 610, 987, 1,597, 2,584, 4,181, 6,765.

Pick up a few pine cones, count the number of spirals, and watch the Fibonacci numbers come up! The illustrations below show you how to count spirals. Counterclockwise, there are 13 spirals, and when you count clockwise, you'll find 8. This particular sequence of numbers pops up in several mathematical formulas and in natural forms such as plants, fruits, and flowers. Why? Well, no one knows! Even today it remains one of the great mysteries of science.

Counterclockwise   **Clockwise**

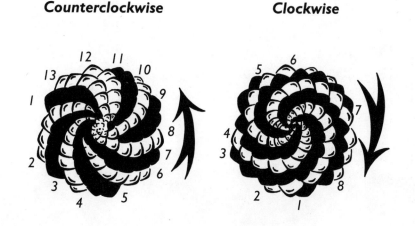

AMAZING math activity

10

Using the table below, can you write the number 1,999 in Roman numerals?

Leonardo Fibonacci helped introduce the number system we use today. Previously, everyone used Roman numerals. Time how long it takes to write 1999 in Roman numerals!

1 = I	18 = XVIII	70 = LXX
2 = II	19 = XIX	80 = LXXX
3 = III	20 = XX	90 = XC
4 = IV	21 = XXI	100 = C
5 = V	22 = XXII	101 = CI
6 = VI	23 = XXIII	102 = CII, etc.
7 = VII	24 = XXIV	200 = CC
8 = VIII	25 = XXV	300 = CCC
9 = IX	26 = XXVI	400 = CD
10 = X	27 = XXVII	500 = D
11 = XI	28 = XXVIII	600 = DC
12 = XII	29 = XXIX	700 = DCC
13 = XIII	30 = XXX	800 = DCCC
14 = XIV	31 = XXXI, etc.	900 = CM
15 = XV	40 = XL	1,000 = M
16 = XVI	50 = L	2,000 = MM
17 = XVII	60 = LX	

The answer is on page 95.

Now that you understand about exponential growth, and you also understand how Fibonacci numbers are generated, try this next activity to put it all together and experience spiral growth on your own.

Build a Spiral with Fibonacci Numbers

You'll need at least 53 counters or markers—jellybeans, pennies, buttons, pebbles, whatever. You can use different types, but be sure they're all about the same size. You'll also need a flat surface, like a tabletop or counter.

0, 1, 1, 2, 3, 5, 8, 13, 21

1. To start the spiral, place one counter on the table. This item represents "1," the first number of the sequence.

2. Place another counter below it. This counter represents the next "1," which is the second number of the sequence.

3. Now place one counter next to the last one to make a line of two counters. This represents the "2," the third number of the sequence.

4. Directly above the "2" line, place two more counters to make a row of three for the "3" line. Just to the left of the "3" line, make a row of five counters for the "5" line.

5. Just below the "5" line, make a row of eight counters. To the right of the eight line, make a row of 13. Directly above the "13" line, make a row of 21. If you have the markers, the time, and the space, you can keep going with this ever-expanding spiral. It just gets bigger and wider!

Note to Reader: After finishing this section, you may never again be able to look at a natural spiral without thinking of exponential growth and Fibonacci numbers!

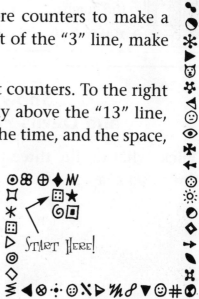

START HERE!

THE MATH GENIUSES

Fibonacci

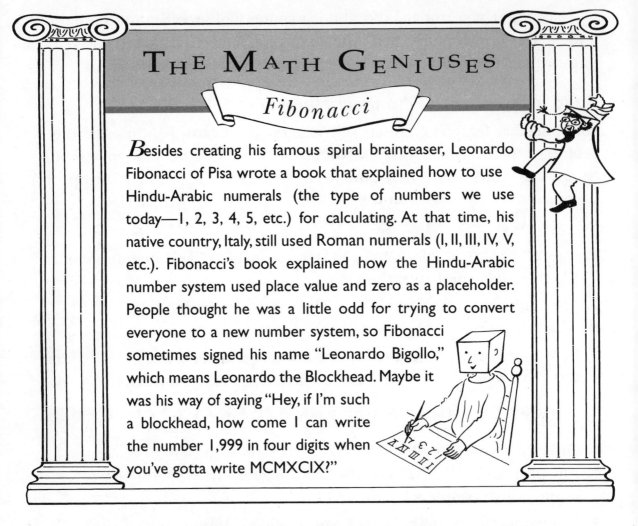

Besides creating his famous spiral brainteaser, Leonardo Fibonacci of Pisa wrote a book that explained how to use Hindu-Arabic numerals (the type of numbers we use today—1, 2, 3, 4, 5, etc.) for calculating. At that time, his native country, Italy, still used Roman numerals (I, II, III, IV, V, etc.). Fibonacci's book explained how the Hindu-Arabic number system used place value and zero as a placeholder. People thought he was a little odd for trying to convert everyone to a new number system, so Fibonacci sometimes signed his name "Leonardo Bigollo," which means Leonardo the Blockhead. Maybe it was his way of saying "Hey, if I'm such a blockhead, how come I can write the number 1,999 in four digits when you've gotta write MCMXCIX?"

Snowflakes, Honeycombs, and Devils Postpile National Monument

Quick, what do the three things listed above have in common? Here's a hint: It's a shape.

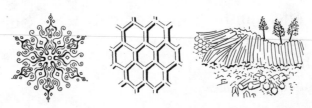

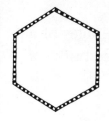

Do you give up? The answer is: They're all hexagons!

A **hexagon** is a **polygon** with six sides. What's a polygon? It's a closed figure made up of line segments. The polygon with the least number of sides is a triangle, with three sides. Next come polygons with four sides. They are called **quadrilaterals**. Squares, **rectangles**, and **parallelograms** are three types of quadrilaterals. Polygons with five sides are called **pentagons**, and as mentioned earlier, a polygon with six sides is called a hexagon.

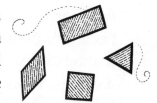

Hexagons are also found in wasps' nests, pineapples, and even in the startling national monument in California called Devils Postpile. In Devils Postpile, hexagonal columns of basalt rock form a 60-foot-high cliff. At the base of the cliff are piles of broken pieces of the columns.

Pentagons occur all the time in nature, too—just slice an apple in half and examine the core (see illustration). If you live in an area where fruit

trees grow, take a look at the flowers on the tree. If it's the tree of an edible fruit, the flowers will always have five petals. When you connect the petal ends from point to point, you'll create a pentagonal shape. When these types of fruit ripen and are finally picked, you'll also see the old petals, or traces of them, at the bottom of the fruit.

AWESOME MATH FACTOIDS

When early settlers who were headed West stopped to rest for the night, they arranged their covered wagons in hexagonal shapes. It enclosed the most possible space and left the least possible area vulnerable to outside attack by hostile groups.

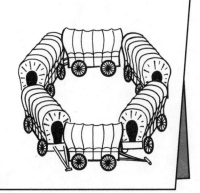

Now, it's easy to see how humans can figure out the advantages of a hexagon, but bees seem to know this instinctively. When a bee builds a honeycomb, it seems to know that hexagonal shapes require the least amount of work. How? Copy this drawing of a honeycomb and you'll see. Did you notice that, once you got going, you had to draw only a few sides of the hexagon since the other sides were already formed by neighboring hexagons? That's the beauty of the hexagon-shaped honeycomb walls. If you were a busy little bee, and you had to keep scraping flakes of beeswax from the underside of your belly to mold the walls, wouldn't you try to make the work as easy as possible and "mind your own beeswax," too?

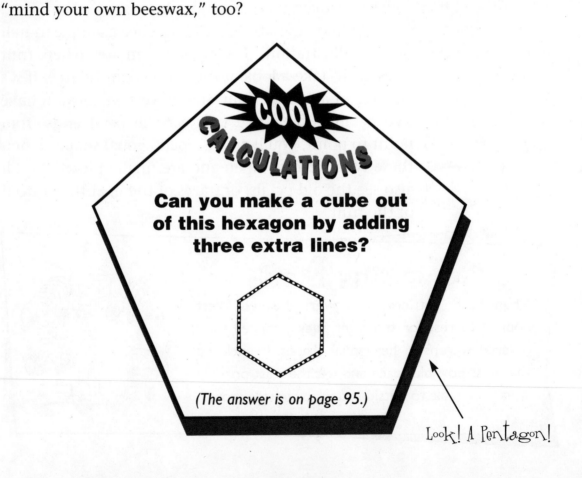

COOL CALCULATIONS

Can you make a cube out of this hexagon by adding three extra lines?

(The answer is on page 95.)

Look! A Pentagon!

Natural Symmetry: It's a Match

When we say something has **symmetry**, we mean it is balanced, or the same on all sides. For example, take a look at the beautiful butterflies at the right. A butterfly is a perfect example of a mathematical idea called **line symmetry**. Something has line symmetry if you can draw a line right down the middle of it and both sides look the

same. Another example might be your reflection on the surface of a pond. See the symmetry of the human body, and draw an imaginary line straight down the middle of your forehead, between your eyes, and downward. You will see that the left side of your body is almost exactly the same as the right side.

Point symmetry is another mathematical idea that shows up in nature. Something has point symmetry if there are many sides that are the same. If it were snowing, and we had a powerful microscope to look at a single snowflake, we would see that even if we turn, or rotate, the snowflake clockwise a little, it still looks like it is right-side-up. Other things found in the natural world that have point symmetry include crystals, starfish, and a variety of flowers and fruit.

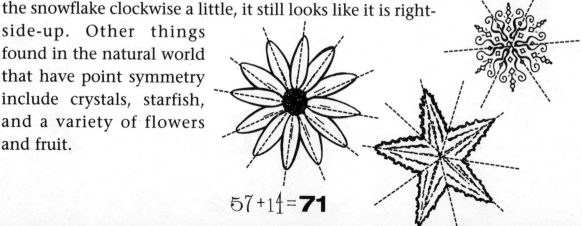

57 + 14 = **71**

COOL MATH
ODDS AND ENDS

From how topology shapes our world to the always incredible Möbius strip, math continues to amaze expert mathematicians, middle school teachers, and brainy kids like you. In this chapter, you'll discover how to play the odds in math and contemplate math's endings. Come to think of it, is there such a thing as math's endings?

The Totally Twisted World of Topology

Geometry is a large branch of math that deals with the shape, size, and position of figures. In geometry, where shapes are very important, a triangle is a triangle, a rectangle is a rectangle, and a square is a square. However, in one branch of mathematics called *topology*, which evolved from geometry, a triangle can also be a rectangle or a square. How? Imagine for a minute that the shapes mentioned above were cut from a stretchy sheet of rubber.

By pulling and distorting the rubber, each shape could be made into another. Because the shapes can become each other with a few tugs here and there, they are considered *topologically equivalent*, or the same. A doughnut and a garden hose are also considered topologically equivalent because they are both objects that have holes in them. Topology challenges the ideas you have about space. It uses mathematical logic to prove that what we find quite unbelievable is, in fact, true. For example, how many sides does a piece of paper have? Two? Think again, and take a look at the Cool Calculations below.

Look! A Parallelogram!

COOL CALCULATIONS

How can a two-sided piece of paper have only one side?

Do you think a strip of paper can have only one side? Yes, if it's a **Möbius strip**! So what's a Möbius strip? Make one yourself and see.

To make your Möbius strip:

1. Cut a strip of paper about 11 inches long and about 1 inch wide.

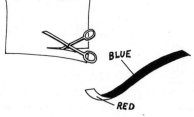

2. Color one side of the paper blue.
Color the other side of the paper red.

3. Give one end of the strip a half-twist, then glue it to the other edge. Allow the glue to dry.

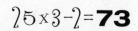

Now, let's say that you, the incredible shrinking math whiz, can shrink down to the size of an ant. Imagine yourself crawling along the blue side of the Möbius strip. Can you do it? What happens?

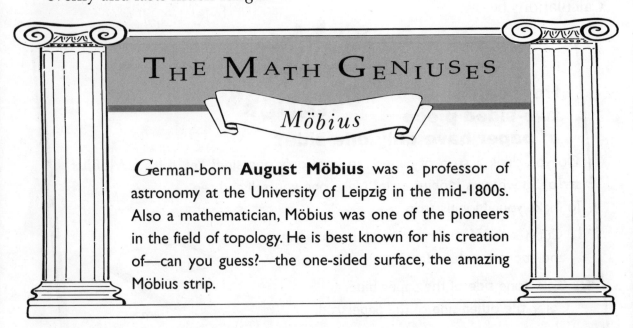

The twist in the strip is what makes the paper one-sided. Although the Möbius strip seems like a purely mathematical and amusing item, it has a practical use, too. For instance, your family car needs a number of fan belts to keep everything running smoothly. If you look closely under the car hood, you'll see that the fan belts have a half twist in them, too. People discovered that when a fan belt, like a Möbius strip, is one-sided, it wears evenly and lasts much longer.

THE MATH GENIUSES

Möbius

German-born **August Möbius** was a professor of astronomy at the University of Leipzig in the mid-1800s. Also a mathematician, Möbius was one of the pioneers in the field of topology. He is best known for his creation of—can you guess?—the one-sided surface, the amazing Möbius strip.

A Topological Magic Trick

This trick is a guaranteed crowd-pleaser! It only takes a little practice to pull it off like a professional magician. Shhh! You're the only one who has to know that the magic lies in the topology of the paper strip.

To make your magic strip:

1. Cut a strip of paper about 2 inches wide and 10 inches long.

2. Curve the paper so it looks like the illustration to the right, then place two paper clips on the strip so they look *exactly* like the ones in the drawing. Show your audience the strip of paper with the paper clips in position. Announce to everyone that you will link both paper clips together—without touching them! The immense power of your mind (well, at least that's what you'll tell everyone) will bend the metal in the paper clips and link them together.

3. Pause a moment, act as if you are concentrating very hard, then, very quickly, pull both edges of the paper outward. (It helps if you hold the paper's edges near the top of the strip and pull so fast and hard that you hear a snapping—not a ripping!—sound.)

4. *Zinggg!* There go the linked paper clips, flying through the air. Have a member of the audience pick them up and bring them back to you as you display the now-linked pair of paper clips. Bravo! (Rub your forehead a little, as if to let everyone know that it was a bit of a strain on the ol' noodle.)

As you can see from the magic trick above, topology is geometry with a twist, a turn, a loop-de-loop, and a triple back flip. It isn't concerned with the shapes or sizes of things. Instead, it focuses on the insides and outsides of things.

At this point, topology is mostly theoretical, meaning that it's not yet useful in the real world, but it has plenty of potential. History has shown us that what starts out as a theory often creates a whole new science. Every

COOL CALCULATIONS

Look! An ellipse!

Can you solve the puzzle of the Königsberg Bridges?

A long time ago, there was an East Prussian town called Königsberg (now the Russian city of Kaliningrad). The city was built along a river that had two islands in the middle of it. These islands were also a part of Königsberg, and the people built seven bridges to get back and forth across the river. Back then, it was the custom to take long walks along the river and see if you could cross each of the seven bridges just once—no doubling back allowed.

When mathematician Leonhard Euler heard about the Königsberg Bridges, he became very interested in solving this popular problem.

Instead of putting on his socks and shoes, he pulled out a pen and paper. He drew a diagram of the town with the bridges. He then tried to trace a path across all seven bridges without lifting his pen. Aha! He had solved the problem.

Do you think it can be done? Trace your finger along the paths and give it a try.

The answer is on page 95.

time you untangle a twisted knot in your shoelaces, you are solving a mathematical, topological puzzle. There is one very famous puzzle, the Königsberg Bridges, having to do with topology. It was finally solved by Leonhard Euler (see his biography on page 31), and he did it, not by taking a stroll, but by stretching his brain!

AMAZING math activity

11

Using only four colors, see if you can make each state a different color from the one bordering it.

Place a sheet of tracing paper over this drawing and trace the outlines of the states. *The answer is on page 95.*

Amazing Math Facts Go Musical!

So you want to grow up to be a world-famous rock star, guitarist, or drummer? If so, you need to hit the math books! Believe it or not, math and music are more related than you may think.

When people clap their hands to the beat of a song, they are actually counting out the beat. When people sing in harmony, they are singing different notes (at the same time) that are related mathematically and therefore sound good together. The beat or rhythm is a mathematical sequence (remember sequences on pages 42–43?) of sounds and silences of different lengths. These sequences are repeated to form a pleasing, predictable pattern (remember patterns on page 34–40?). Hmm. It seems there's more to music and mathematics than meets the ear! Rock on—uh, *read* on—for more on how music meets math!

Say you're onstage inside a huge sports arena. The lights go down. The crowd cheers. You strap on your electric guitar and prepare to blast the audience with some seriously blistering guitar sounds. You play one note—a "C"—and let the sound hang in the air. Because you've studied music for many years, you know that this note vibrates at exactly 264 vibrations a second. The crowd screams its approval as you and your band launch into one of your favorite songs. As you play, every squealing note you coax out of your guitar vibrates at a different rate. It is the arrangement of these vibrations that make music—whether it's heavy metal, hip-hop, reggae, classical, rhythm and blues, or easy listening (yeah, sure).

Pythagorus (see his biography on pages 10–11) and his followers were the first people to link mathematics with music. They believed that the distance from planet Earth to each individual star or planet was like the string on an instrument. When the stars orbited around Earth, these "strings" were shortened or lengthened, and thus created changing, harmonious sounds (think school choir on a really BIG stage), or what he called "the music of the spheres." Pythagorus said that this musical harmony was continuous and people could not hear it because they were so used to it.

In 1618, Johannes Kepler, a German astronomer, attempted to connect the speed at which planets moved to the musical scale. He published his findings in *Harmony of the World*. While Kepler's studies led to significant discoveries in astronomy, there is no scientific evidence of the astronomy-music connection today.

The Math Geniuses

Einstein

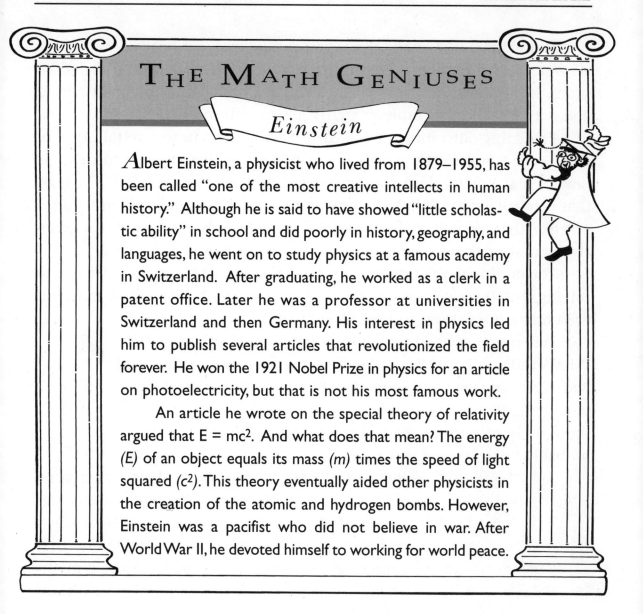

Albert Einstein, a physicist who lived from 1879–1955, has been called "one of the most creative intellects in human history." Although he is said to have showed "little scholastic ability" in school and did poorly in history, geography, and languages, he went on to study physics at a famous academy in Switzerland. After graduating, he worked as a clerk in a patent office. Later he was a professor at universities in Switzerland and then Germany. His interest in physics led him to publish several articles that revolutionized the field forever. He won the 1921 Nobel Prize in physics for an article on photoelectricity, but that is not his most famous work.

An article he wrote on the special theory of relativity argued that $E = mc^2$. And what does that mean? The energy *(E)* of an object equals its mass *(m)* times the speed of light squared *(c^2)*. This theory eventually aided other physicists in the creation of the atomic and hydrogen bombs. However, Einstein was a pacifist who did not believe in war. After World War II, he devoted himself to working for world peace.

Heads or Tails? Adventures in Probability

When you flip a coin, do you always choose heads? Or do you choose tails? If you flipped the coin 20 times, do you think you'd get heads most of the time, or tails? Or would you get heads half the time and tails the other half? Try this experiment and see for yourself.

$$9+8+9+10+11+12+20 = \mathbf{79}$$

Write down how many times you think you'll get heads or tails. This is your prediction. Flip a quarter or, if you're feeling cheap, a nickel 20 times. Write down how many times you got heads and how many times you got tails. Did the results match your prediction?

Predicting outcomes of a tossed coin introduces us to a certain type of math called **probability**, which is just a fancy-schmancy way to describe how to make pretty darn-good guesses. The science of probability tells us that you will get heads half the time and tails half the time. When put into practice, though, you could flip a coin and get heads every time. The probability of something is just what is likely to—or will *probably*—happen.

You do this all the time in your head and probably don't realize you're solving a mathematical problem. Maybe you even did it the last time you tried to guess what was in your lunch bag.

When you opened your lunch bag, you saw a sandwich. What kind was it? Well, you figured, two days before that you had liver sausage, and one day before that you had liver sausage. Last week you had liver sausage all five days. You thought hard and decided that today's sandwich would probably be liver sausage, too.

But wait. Could you be sure? Hadn't Dad gone grocery shopping yesterday? Didn't you see a big jar of peanut butter—extra crunchy—on the kitchen counter this morning? What is the probability that you might get liver sausage today? Expressed mathematically, it would look like a **ratio** or a fraction, respectively:

$$1 : 2 \text{ or } \tfrac{1}{2}$$

The ratio shows there was a one-in-two chance that you would have gotten liver sausage, but there was also a one-in-two chance that you would have gotten peanut butter. Those are pretty good chances, otherwise known as "fifty-fifty."

Now, what if there was a container of freshly made egg salad in the refrigerator? What were your chances of getting liver sausage again?

1 : 3 or **⅓**

One in three. Still a pretty good chance.

Okay, now let's say that not only was there peanut butter and egg salad to consider, but also turkey, tuna salad, Swiss cheese, and pimento loaf. What were your chances of getting liver sausage?

1 : 7 or **⅐**

At that point, your chance of getting liver sausage was beginning to look pretty slim. Hurrah!

COOL CALCULATIONS

Can you calculate the probability of drawing the following four cards?

Remember, there are 52 cards in a deck, 4 suits of 13 cards each, 26 red cards, and 26 black.

1. What are your chances of drawing a red card?

2. What are your chances of drawing a heart?

3. What are your chances of drawing an ace?

4. What are your chances of drawing the ace of hearts?

Try to keep this in mind the next time you play cards. Play the odds, meaning: Know what your chances are first!

The answers and an explanation of how it works are on page 95.

Look! A Square!

Basketball Statistics and How to Read Them

When you watch a basketball game on TV, do you ever wonder why you see a row of numbers across the bottom of the screen just when your favorite player is trying to sink a free throw? These numbers are called *statistics*. They're simply information about the player's performance.

Let's take a look at the following basketball statistics:

- **FG 12–19** means the player made 12 out of 19 field goal attempts.

- **FT 2–8** means the player made 2 free throws out of 8 attempts.

Now, when you look at statistics for the season *average*, you'll see numbers like this:

FG% .620

What that means is based on the number of field goals the player has attempted during the season, she or he is scoring 62 percent of them (which is pretty good).

If the player's FT% (free throw average) is .500, that's not so good. He or she is nailing, on the average, only one half of his or her free throw attempts.

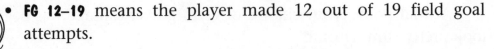

EXCELLENT equations to Know & Love

To find the average of something, look below!

If a player made 26 points during one game, 13 during another, and 23 during another, what would be the average points he or she made per game?

Add up the points: **26 + 13 + 23 = 62**

Divide by the number of games (in this case, 3): so **62 ÷ 3**

And you get the average number of points per game: **20.6**

Total points ÷ number of games = average number of points per game

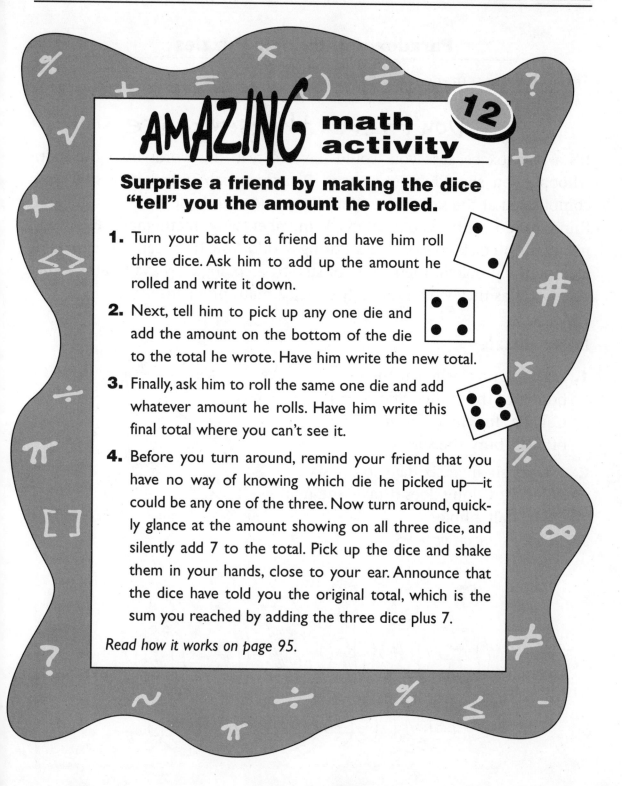

AMAZING math activity

12

Surprise a friend by making the dice "tell" you the amount he rolled.

1. Turn your back to a friend and have him roll three dice. Ask him to add up the amount he rolled and write it down.

2. Next, tell him to pick up any one die and add the amount on the bottom of the die to the total he wrote. Have him write the new total.

3. Finally, ask him to roll the same one die and add whatever amount he rolls. Have him write this final total where you can't see it.

4. Before you turn around, remind your friend that you have no way of knowing which die he picked up—it could be any one of the three. Now turn around, quickly glance at the amount showing on all three dice, and silently add 7 to the total. Pick up the dice and shake them in your hands, close to your ear. Announce that the dice have told you the original total, which is the sum you reached by adding the three dice plus 7.

Read how it works on page 95.

Paradoxes and Logic Puzzles

The following sentence is: a **paradox**:

Don't read this sentence.

It's a paradox because you would have to read the words to know that, whoops, you shouldn't read them! Paradoxes can sound very silly and complicated at the same time. It all has to do with logic, which has everything to do with mathematics. Remember why mathematicians were recruited to crack enemy codes during World War II? Because they could analyze the problem, then think of step-by-step, logical ways to attack the code—just as they would logically attack a math problem.

Logic Puzzles

1. An airplane crashed at the border of the United States and Canada. In which country did officials bury the survivors?

2. It takes six men six days to dig six holes. How long does it take one man to dig half a hole?

The answers are on page 95.

336÷4=**84**

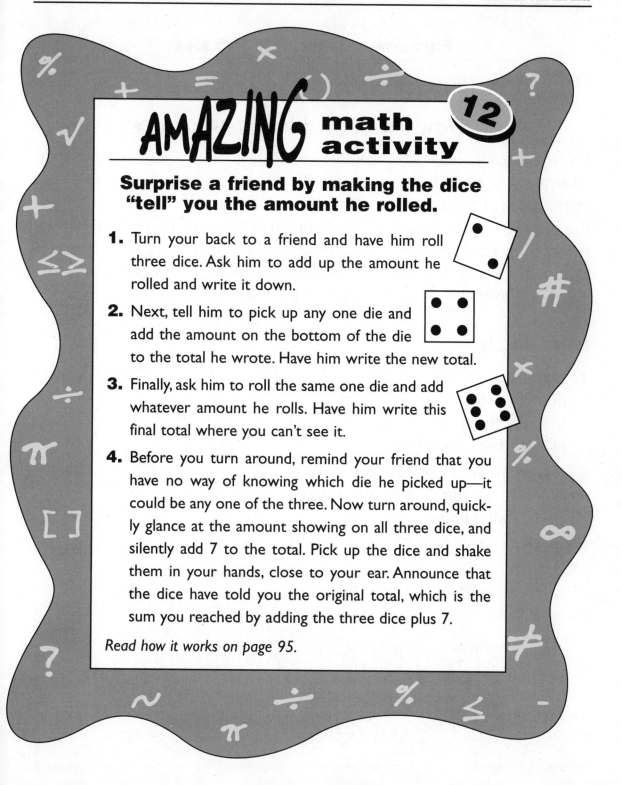

AMAZING math activity

12

Surprise a friend by making the dice "tell" you the amount he rolled.

1. Turn your back to a friend and have him roll three dice. Ask him to add up the amount he rolled and write it down.

2. Next, tell him to pick up any one die and add the amount on the bottom of the die to the total he wrote. Have him write the new total.

3. Finally, ask him to roll the same one die and add whatever amount he rolls. Have him write this final total where you can't see it.

4. Before you turn around, remind your friend that you have no way of knowing which die he picked up—it could be any one of the three. Now turn around, quickly glance at the amount showing on all three dice, and silently add 7 to the total. Pick up the dice and shake them in your hands, close to your ear. Announce that the dice have told you the original total, which is the sum you reached by adding the three dice plus 7.

Read how it works on page 95.

Paradoxes and Logic Puzzles

The following sentence is: a **paradox**:

Don't read this sentence.

It's a paradox because you would have to read the words to know that, whoops, you shouldn't read them! Paradoxes can sound very silly and complicated at the same time. It all has to do with logic, which has every-thing to do with mathematics. Remember why mathematicians were recruited to crack enemy codes during World War II? Because they could analyze the problem, then think of step-by-step, logical ways to attack the code—just as they would logically attack a math problem.

Logic Puzzles

1. An airplane crashed at the border of the United States and Canada. In which country did officials bury the survivors?

2. It takes six men six days to dig six holes. How long does it take one man to dig half a hole?

The answers are on page 95.

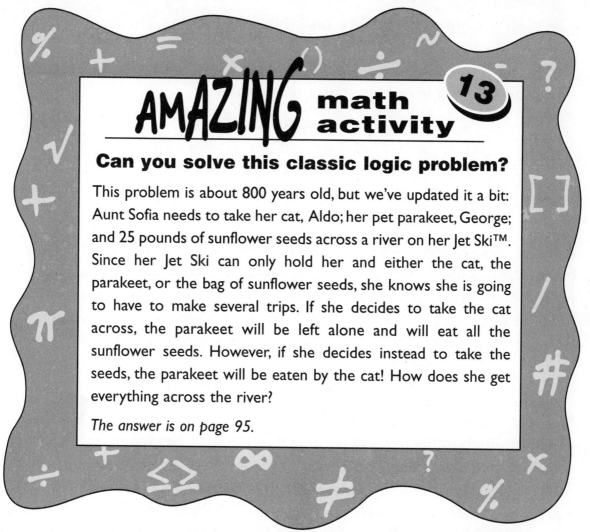

AMAZING math activity 13

Can you solve this classic logic problem?

This problem is about 800 years old, but we've updated it a bit: Aunt Sofia needs to take her cat, Aldo; her pet parakeet, George; and 25 pounds of sunflower seeds across a river on her Jet Ski™. Since her Jet Ski can only hold her and either the cat, the parakeet, or the bag of sunflower seeds, she knows she is going to have to make several trips. If she decides to take the cat across, the parakeet will be left alone and will eat all the sunflower seeds. However, if she decides instead to take the seeds, the parakeet will be eaten by the cat! How does she get everything across the river?

The answer is on page 95.

Stretch Your Mind!: Chaos and the Butterfly Effect

The **Butterfly Effect**, named by meteorologist **Edward Lorenz** in 1963, is what happens when a very small change in one situation causes an unpredictable change in another. For example, let's say that right now a delicate butterfly is fluttering its wings over a field of flowers somewhere on the other side of the world. According to **chaos theory**, the butterfly's wings create a minuscule amount of air turbulence that could multiply erratically over time and space to the point where a huge storm system breaks out somewhere on this side of the world. The official name for this "butterfly

$25 + 25 + 25 + 10 = \textbf{85}$

effect" is "sensitive dependence on initial conditions." The resulting disorder is called *chaos*, which is the opposite of order.

In his book *Chaos: Making a New Science*, James Gleick uses the following folk rhyme to help illustrate the subject:

> *For want of a nail, the shoe was lost;*
> *For want of a shoe, the horse was lost;*
> *For want of a horse, the rider was lost;*
> *For want of a rider, the battle was lost;*
> *For want of a battle, the kingdom was lost!*

Because of one small missing nail, a whole kingdom was destroyed in battle! Who could predict such a huge outcome? Nobody, and that's what makes chaos theory so difficult to study—the results are totally unpredictable. Can you think of an action no matter how small and predict the future consequences of this action? Let your imagination go!

Infinity: The Ultimate Mind Game

The idea of an infinite number is a paradox because there is no such thing as an infinite number. **Infinity** is not a number. It is an *ever-expanding idea*. Infinity is not a *something*. It can't really *be* anywhere, either, except in your mind, which is where all your *ideas* about mathematics exist.

In her one-woman play, *The Search for Intelligent Life in the Universe*, comic Lily Tomlin describes infinity as a box of Cream of Wheat. The man on the box is holding a box of Cream of Wheat, which shows him holding a box of Cream of Wheat, and so on, and so on. . . . The idea of infinity is one of endless expansion. But it doesn't have to take up a lot of space. For example, one Greek philosopher offered a paradox about infinity that illustrates endless expansion in a very small place. Let's say you need to walk across your school playground. You will never get across if you travel in the following way (keeping in mind you are always moving forward, never standing still): First walk halfway across, then pause. Then walk half of that distance forward and pause again. Then walk half of that distance forward. Keep going, moving only half the distance you moved the previous time. Guess what? You will *never* get across the playground. Infinity doesn't necessarily have to expand. It only has to go on forever.

We see the results of mathematical relationships all around us, in the patterns of nature and in the way certain games are won or lost. We see the awesome high-tech machines we've created. We see the funny ways certain numbers behave when you add, subtract, multiply, or divide them on paper. Sometimes we have to stop ourselves and understand that the numbers themselves are only symbols for ideas. You can't really *see* 3, or 378. Neither can you *see* zero. You can't *see* infinity either, but the symbol looks like this:

The next time you're stumped by a math problem, calculation, trick, activity, or idea, remember this: Math is, always has been, and always will be totally logical. And guess what? So are you! You were born that way—your brain is wired that way. It's sort of like being "cable-ready" so that you're all set up for math, mathematical ideas, and mathematical success!

Math History at a Glance

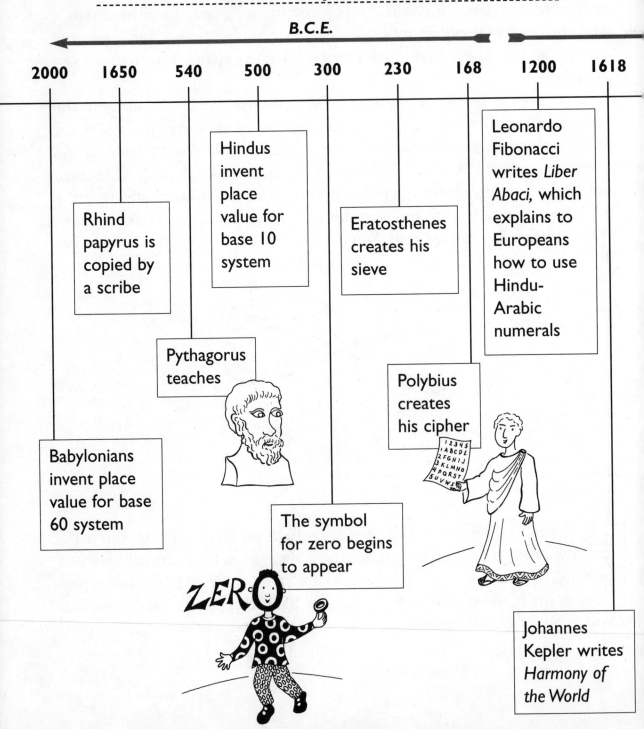

B.C.E.

| 2000 | 1650 | 540 | 500 | 300 | 230 | 168 | 1200 | 1618 |

Rhind papyrus is copied by a scribe

Hindus invent place value for base 10 system

Eratosthenes creates his sieve

Leonardo Fibonacci writes *Liber Abaci*, which explains to Europeans how to use Hindu-Arabic numerals

Pythagorus teaches

Polybius creates his cipher

Babylonians invent place value for base 60 system

The symbol for zero begins to appear

ZERO

Johannes Kepler writes *Harmony of the World*

8 x 11 = **88**

pause. Then walk half of that distance forward and pause again. Then walk half of that distance forward. Keep going, moving only half the distance you moved the previous time. Guess what? You will *never* get across the playground. Infinity doesn't necessarily have to expand. It only has to go on forever.

We see the results of mathematical relationships all around us, in the patterns of nature and in the way certain games are won or lost. We see the awesome high-tech machines we've created. We see the funny ways certain numbers behave when you add, subtract, multiply, or divide them on paper. Sometimes we have to stop ourselves and understand that the numbers themselves are only symbols for ideas. You can't really *see* 3, or 378. Neither can you *see* zero. You can't *see* infinity either, but the symbol looks like this:

The next time you're stumped by a math problem, calculation, trick, activity, or idea, remember this: Math is, always has been, and always will be totally logical. And guess what? So are you! You were born that way—your brain is wired that way. It's sort of like being "cable-ready" so that you're all set up for math, mathematical ideas, and mathematical success!

Math History at a Glance

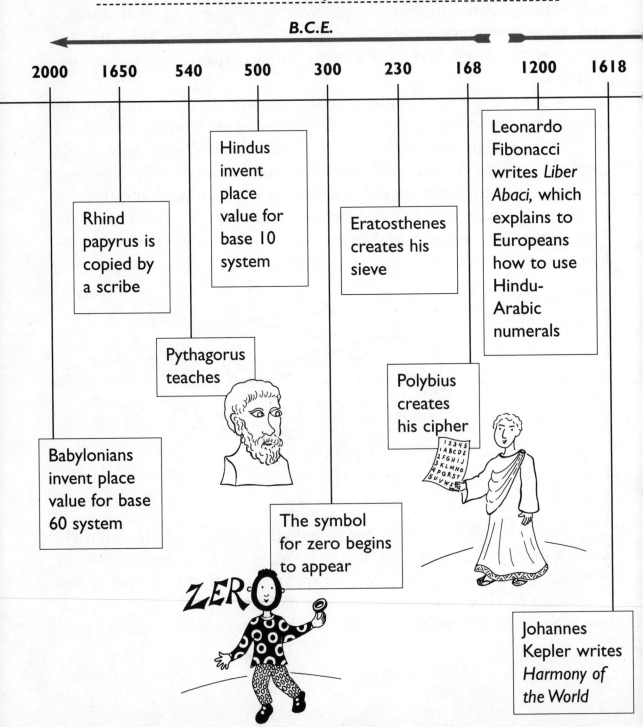

B.C.E.

2000 1650 540 500 300 230 168 1200 1618

Rhind papyrus is copied by a scribe

Hindus invent place value for base 10 system

Pythagorus teaches

Eratosthenes creates his sieve

Leonardo Fibonacci writes *Liber Abaci,* which explains to Europeans how to use Hindu-Arabic numerals

Polybius creates his cipher

Babylonians invent place value for base 60 system

The symbol for zero begins to appear

ZERO

Johannes Kepler writes *Harmony of the World*

$8 \times 11 = 88$

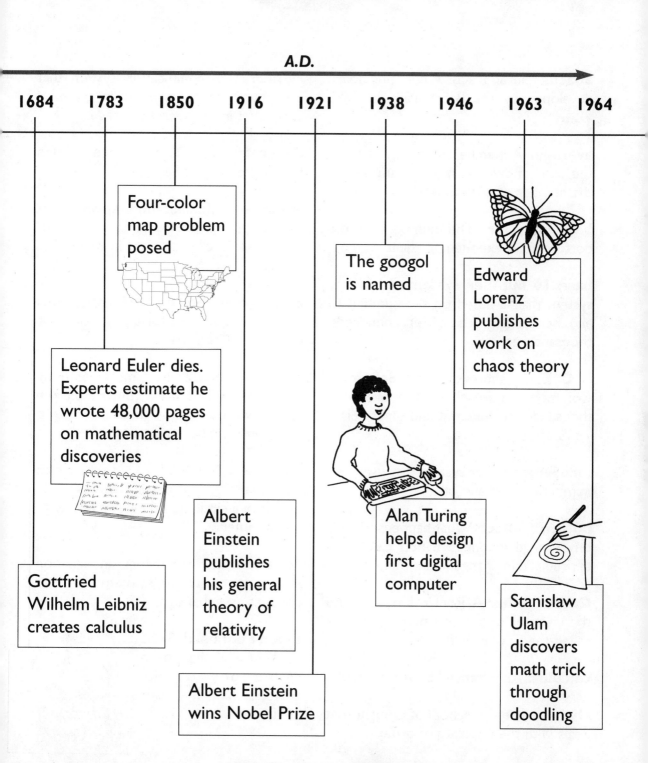

A.D.

| 1684 | 1783 | 1850 | 1916 | 1921 | 1938 | 1946 | 1963 | 1964 |

Four-color map problem posed

The googol is named

Edward Lorenz publishes work on chaos theory

Leonard Euler dies. Experts estimate he wrote 48,000 pages on mathematical discoveries

Albert Einstein publishes his general theory of relativity

Alan Turing helps design first digital computer

Gottfried Wilhelm Leibniz creates calculus

Albert Einstein wins Nobel Prize

Stanislaw Ulam discovers math trick through doodling

500÷5-11=**89**

GLOSSARY

abacus (plural, abaci): A counting board developed by the Babylonians in 1795 B.C.E.

average: A number found by dividing the sum of two or more quantities by the number of quantities.

base number: The number on the bottom in an exponential equation.

base 10 number system: A number system that is based on the number 10 and increasing groups of tens, hundreds, thousands, etc.

B. C. E.: An abbreviation for Before the Common Era, which started over one thousand nine hundred and ninety-eight years ago.

binary: A number system that uses two numbers—zero and one.

butterfly effect: What happens when a tiny change in one situation causes an unpredictable change in another.

Caesar, Julius: A Roman emperor and the inventor of a secret message cipher called the Caesar Shift.

calculus: An advanced branch of math.

chaos theory: A school of thought that deals with the opposite of order.

cipher: A communication system that uses numbers or symbols in place of each *letter* in the secret message.

circumference: The distance around the outside edge of a circle.

code: A communication system that uses substitute words, numbers, or symbols in place of each *word* in the secret message.

cryptanalyst: Someone who specializes in cryptanalysis, the solving of codes or ciphers; a code breaker.

cryptography: Writing messages using secret codes. This word comes from the Greek words *kryptos,* meaning secret, and *graphos,* meaning writing.

diameter: The width of a circle, which is a line segment passing through the center of a circle that connects one edge to the other.

equation: In mathematics, an equation is a mathematical statement that contains an equal sign.

Euler, Leonhard: Swiss thinker who has been called one of the greatest mathematicians in history.

Euler circles: See "Venn diagram." Although Leibniz and Euler also used circle diagrams, John Venn's name is the one that has stuck.

exponent: A number written just above and to the right of a base number representing the number of times the base is to be multiplied by itself.

exponential growth: A very rapid increase or development. This is shown in the Fibonacci sequence.

extrapolate: To predict by referring to known data. In math, you can extrapolate what comes before or after a sequence by looking at the existing numbers.

factor: A number that divides evenly into another number.

Fibonacci, Leonardo: Italian mathematician who advocated the use of Hindu-Arabic numerals and discovered the Fibonacci sequence.

Fibonacci sequence: A pattern of numbers often found in nature.

fraction: A fraction is made up of two numbers. The bottom number represents the whole number, while the top number stands for a part of that whole number. Fractions are often used to show a part of the whole.

geometry: A large branch of math that deals with the shape, size, and position of figures.

googol: A number one with 100 zeros written after it. A googol can also be written as the number 10^{100} in exponential form.

googolplex: A googolplex is a number one with a googol of zeros after it, also written as the number 10^{googol} or $10^{10^{100}}$ in exponential form.

hexagon: A polygon with six sides.

infinity: That which is endless, unlimited, or ever-expanding. ∞

integer: A whole number value that is either negative, positive, or zero.

intersection: The area where two sets cross over each other.

irrational number: A number that can't be expressed exactly, either as a fraction or a whole number.

key: In coding, a key matches up the coded words or letters with the actual words or letters, allowing the secret message to be cracked.

Leibniz, Gottfried Wilhelm: The inventor of the binary system and calculus.

line symmetry: When a line can be drawn down the middle of an object and both sides look the same.

Lorenz, Edward: A meteorologist who is responsible for bringing the butterfly effect to the world of mathematics.

Möbius, August: The creator of the one-sided surface, the Möbius strip.

Möbius strip: A loop with a half twist that has only one side.

negative number: A number that is less than zero. To show that it's negative, a minus sign is written before it.

palindrome: A word or number that reads the same, forward and backward.

paradox: A statement that seems to contradict itself.

parallelogram: A four-sided shape with equal opposite sides.

pattern: A group of numbers that are related in a predictable way.

pattern of consecutive sums: When the last two numbers of a sequence are added together to get the next number. The pattern goes on and on.

pentagon: A polygon with five sides.

perfect number: A number whose factors add up to itself.

pi: Pi (π) is the 16th letter of the Greek alphabet, and it stands for the ratio of the circumference of a circle to its diameter, which is approximately 3.1415926535.

place value: The value of the place of a digit within a number.

point symmetry: When an object has many sides that are exactly the same.

polygon: A closed figure made up of line segments.

Polybius: A Greek historian who created a cipher square to send secret messages.

prime number: A number that can be divided only by the number one and itself.

probability: The science of predicting.

product: A number that results when two or more numbers are multiplied together.

Pythagorus: A Greek philosopher and mathematician born around 580 B.C.E. He believed that everything in the world could be expressed in numbers.

quadrilateral: A four-sided shape.

radius: A straight line from the center of a circle to any point on the circle's edge.

ratio: A comparison in number or quantity between two things.

rational number: A number that can be expressed as a fraction or whole number.

rectangle: A four-sided polygon with four right angles, where opposite sides are equal in length.

remainder: The amount left over after division that is less than the factor.

rhombus: A parallelogram with four equal sides.

Roman numerals: The Roman numbering system, written in letters. (See page 66 to see many of the numbers.)

sequence: A set of numbers that come one after another, arranged in a certain order.

set: A group of objects or numbers that are related in some way or have similar qualities.

spirals: An example from nature that describes the mathematical idea of exponential growth.

square: A polygon with four right angles and four equal sides.

square number: The result when a number is multiplied by itself.

statistics: A branch of math that deals with the analysis of all sorts of groups of numbers (seen often in sports).

subset: A set within a larger set.

symmetry: When a picture or an object is equal on both sides of an imaginary line.

topology: A branch of geometry that deals with shapes and surfaces.

triangle: A polygon with three sides.

triangle number: Any quantity that can be arranged into rows that gradually increase by one.

Turing, Alan: English math scholar who helped crack the German Enigma code. He also created an early computer prototype, the "Turing machine."

Ulam, Stanislaw: A mathematician who discovered a way of finding prime numbers through his doodling.

Venn diagram: A type of graph that uses intersecting circles to show the relationships between sets.

Venn, John: A British teacher who created the Venn diagram.

vigesimal system: The base 5 number system used by Mayan Indians.

whole number: A number that contains no fractional value.

zero: The absence of quantity.

page 7: One. Only the speaker is going to St. Ives!

page 25: Amazing Math Activity # 2
It's 28. The sum of all its divisors —1, 2, 4, 7, and 14.

page 28: Amazing Math Activity # 3
15, 21, 28, 36, 45, and 55

page 29: Cool Calculations
No, consecutive numbers do not add up to square numbers, nor do consecutive even numbers. You can only get a square number by adding consecutive *odd* numbers.
36 or 6^2, 49 or 7^2, 64 or 8^2, 81 or 9^2, 100 or 10^2

page 37:　　　e. 11,111　　g. 1,111,111
　　　　　　　f. 111,111　　h. 11,111,111

page 41: Amazing Math Activity # 6

x	2	3	x	5	x	7	x	x	x
11	x	13	x	x	x	17	x	19	x
x	x	23	x	x	x	x	x	29	x
31	x	x	x	x	x	37	x	x	x
41	x	43	x	x	x	47	x	x	x
x	x	53	x	x	x	x	x	59	x
61	x	x	x	x	x	67	x	x	x
71	x	73	x	x	x	x	x	79	x
x	x	83	x	x	x	x	x	89	x
x	x	x	x	x	97	x	x	x	

page 56: Amazing Math Activity # 8
YOU'RE A BRAIN.

page 57: The thought bubble reads: I PREFER ANCHOVIES ON MY CAESAR! The secret message reads: WHAT'S UP, CAESAR?

page 62: Amazing Math Activity # 9
A STICK.

page 64: Cool Calculations
.01 + .01 = .02
.02 + .02 = .04
.04 + .04 = .08
.08 + .08 = .16
.16 + .16 = .32
.32 + .32 = .64
.64 + .64 = 1.28
1.28 + 1.28 = 2.56
2.56 + 2.56 = 5.12
5.12 + 5.12 = 10.24
10.24 + 10.24 = 20.48
20.48 + 20.48 = 40.96
40.96 + 40.96 = 81.92
81.92 + 81.92 =163.84
163.84 +163.84 = 327.68
327.68 + 327.68 = 655.36
655.36 + 655.36 = 1,310.72
1,310.72 +1,310.72 = 2,621.44
2,621.44 + 2,621.44 = 5,242.88
5,242.88 + 5,242.88 = 10,485.76
10,485.76 + 10,485.76 = 20,971.52
20,971.52 + 20,971.52 = 41,943.04
41,943.04 + 41,943.04 = 83,886.08
83,886.08 + 83,886.08 = 167,772.16
167,772.16 + 167,772.16 = 335,544.32
335,544.32 + 335,544.32 = 671,088.64
671,088.64 + 671,088.64 = 1,342,177.28

page 66: Amazing Math Activity # 10
MCMXCIX.

page 70: Cool Calculations

page 76: Cool Calculations
Euler's connect-the-dots diagram saved everyone in the town a lot of blisters and sore feet by proving that it was *impossible* to cross each bridge only once. Psych!

page 77: Amazing Math Activity # 11
No matter how complicated a map is, the mapmaker needs only four colors to define each area. This problem was first stated in 1850. However, mathematicians could not prove that this would always be true—then came the computer. In 1976, math professors Kenneth Appel and Wolfgang Haken at the University of Illinois proved, mathematically, that four colors are all that are needed. It took computers approximately 1,200 hours to generate the mathematical proof. Take a look at any globe or atlas to see for yourself!

page 81: Cool Calculations
1. Since you know that half the cards are red, the ratio would be 26:52, or 26 red cards out of 52 total cards. Then you can simplify that number down by dividing by common divisors (in this case, 26). The final answer is 1:2. Some people call this "2 to 1 odds."

2. With 13 hearts in a deck, the ratio is 13:52. After putting this in fraction form, 13/52, and reducing this fraction to its least common multiples, you get 1/4. The odds are 4 to 1.

3. With four aces in a deck, the ratio is 4:52. Put it into fraction form and reduce the fraction, which gives you 1/13. The odds are 13 to 1.

4. 1:52. Talk about a long shot. This one's a *very* long shot. Good luck!

page 83: Amazing Math Activity # 12
Opposite sides of a die always total seven. When your friend looked at the bottom of one die and added it to the total, he "eliminated" that die altogether. When he rolled the die a second time and it appeared with all the others, all you had to do was add 7 to whatever amount appeared on all three dice.

pages 84: Logic Puzzles
1. If your answer is "none," you are absolutely right. Survivors are people who survive, or live through, a crash. They're not dead. And you can only bury dead people.

2. You can't dig half a hole. A hole is a hole is a hole.

page 85: Amazing Math Activity # 13
First she takes the parakeet. Then she returns to pick up the cat. She drops off the cat and takes the parakeet back. She picks up the bag of sunflower seeds and leaves the parakeet. Finally, she returns to get the parakeet.